# A
# REASON
# FOR
# LIVING

# A
# REASON
# FOR
# LIVING

*George Roche*

*Foreword by George Gilder*

**REGNERY GATEWAY**

*Washington, D.C.*

Library of Congress Cataloging-in-Publication Data

Roche, George Charles.
A reason for living / George C. Roche : foreword by George Gilder.
p.   cm.
Contents: Jocko coyle—A job to be done—Adobe Park—The Courtship of Dominic Belmonte—A helping hand—Things used to be simpler—St. Elmo—Ground blizzard.
ISBN 0-89526-545-1
1. Rocky Mountains—Fiction.   I. Title.
PS3568.O323R4   1990

813'.54—dc20                                                    89-36663
                                                               CIP

Published in the United States by
Regnery Gateway
1130 17th Street, NW
Washington, DC 20036

Distributed to the trade by
National Book Network
4720-A Boston Way
Lanham, MD 20706

Manufactured in the United States of America

10  9  8  7  6  5  4  3  2  1

TO MY FATHER,
WHO ALWAYS HAD A REASON FOR LIVING

# Contents

# Foreword

A Harvard-trained economist talking about the rough-and-tumble early years of Colorado sounds, even to my ears, somewhat awry, but despite my years in Cambridge—or perhaps because of them—my heart has long been elsewhere, in places like Hillsdale with the courageous and visionary battle that George Roche has waged to preserve the values of a true American education against educational and legal bureaucracies run amok.

When *Going Home*, the volume which inspired the collection of short stories here, first appeared, my wife and I read it aloud, and, for the first time, I felt I better understood the source of George Roche's vision and courage. I was grateful to him for telling us about those people and places he knows so well. Even though I am a Modern Man—that is to say, I spend most of my time flying around the world in 747s and writing about the latest technological innovation or market trend—I am also something of an anachronism. I live on a farm in rural Massachusetts, surrounded by the hills my family has worked for generations and I understand that the most advanced new technologies spring from the same freedom and faith that George Roche proclaims, teaches, and ex-emplifies.

In an age when it is fashionable to search for roots, I don't have to go further than my own backyard. And neither does George Roche, for whom the past is a living and breathing part of the present. Here he offers you some descriptions of the men and women of the West in the early-to-mid-years of this century, people who shared a simple creed and no small amount of guts and determination. More than ever, in an age when this combination of faith and character seem to be in short supply, we need to listen to what he is saying: that there is a reason for living and that this reason lies outside material desires. He writes in a clean and simple style, but there is a touch of the legendary Angel of Shavano (so named for one of the peaks high in the Rockies where he was raised) in George Roche's prose and vision. His homely tales can rise suddenly to snow-capped heights of poetic philosophy and Christian truth.

These are explicitly Christian stories, but some believers won't be comfortable with the hard-drinking, hard-living brand of Christianity the stories' main characters display. As it happens, though, they are much like real men and women who find the spiral road to Heaven to be full of tortuous twists and turns, but always leading upward if one has the courage and the conviction to follow.

*A Reason for Living* also celebrates what used to be called "the pioneer spirit." Some years ago, I wrote a book on capitalism that attempted to celebrate that same spirit from a different perspective. The concluding chapter noted that all human pioneers, from poets and composers in their many epiphanies to scientists on the mystical frontiers of matter where life again begins, are essentially engaged in forms of devotion. All knowledge of living and growing things (concepts and economies) is partly subjective and intuitive and thus mystically dependent on the ideas of others and on the worship, however unconscious, of God. God is the foundation of all living knowledge; and the human mind, to the extent it can know anything beyond its own meager reach, partakes of the mind of God. In *A Reason for Living*, George Roche never wanders far from this foundation.

In the United States today we are facing the usual calculus of impossibility, recited by the familiar aspirants to a master plan. It is said we must abandon economic freedom because our frontier is closed; because our biosphere is strained; because our resources are running out; because our technology is perverse; because our population rises; because our horizons are closing in. We walk, it is said, in a shadow of death, with depleted air, poisoned earth and water, and a fallout of explosive growth showering from the clouds of our future in a quiet carcinogenic rain. In this extremity, we cannot afford the luxuries of competition and waste and freedom. We have reached the end of the open road; we are beating against the gates of an occluded frontier. We must tax and regulate and plan, redistribute our wealth and ration our consumption, because we have reached the end of openness, so the planners say.

But quite to the contrary, as George Roche has demonstrated in his own lifetime, these problems and crises are in themselves the new frontier; are themselves the mandate for individual and corporate competition and creativity; are themselves the reason why we cannot afford the consolations of planning and stasis. The old frontier of the American West also appeared closed at first. It became an open reservoir of wealth only in retrospect, because people like those in George's stories dared to risk their lives and families in the quest for riches, looking for gold (of which there was relatively little in the United States) and finding oil (then of little use). Only in retrospect were the barrens of Texas and Oklahoma an energy cornucopia, the flat prairies a breadbasket for the world, or Thomas Edison a catalytic genius and Henry Ford the savior of capitalism in the grips of an earlier closing circle. The future is forever incalculable; only in freedom can its challenges be mastered.

The economists who make the case for stasis and planning in these terms formulate point by point the case against themselves. The closing circle, the resource crisis, the thermal threat, the nuclear peril, the "graying" of technology, the population advance, the famine factor, and whatever else is new in the perennial jeremiad of the rational budgeteer and actuary of our fate—all these conditions are themselves the mandate for *A Reason for Living*'s affirmation of the ingenuity of free and God-fearing men.

Understanding this will allow us to see the best way of helping the poor and of recognizing truths of equality before God that can only come from freedom and diversity on earth. It will lead us to abandon, above all, the idea that the human race can become self-sufficient, can separate itself from chance and fortune in a hubristic siege of rational resource management, income distribution, and futuristic planning. Our greatest and only resource is the miracle of human creativity in a relation of openness to the divine.

The tale of human life is less the pageant of unfolding rationality and purpose envisaged by the Enlightenment than a saga of desert wanderings and brief bounty, the endless dialogue between man and God, between alienation and providence, as we search for the ever-rising and receding promised land, which we can see most clearly, with the most luminous logic, when we have the faith and courage to leave ourselves open to chance and fate.

So come with George Roche to the shadow of Mt. Shavano, where the snow piles up over the rooftops and animals howl in the night and the road is closed for the season and even though your old friend drinks too much sometimes late at night, that is the time when he may have important truths to share, so you'd better listen. And then perhaps you'll know why Hillsdale is a better place than Harvard and why George Roche is a national treasure.

George Gilder
Tyringham, Massachusetts

# *Preface*

Many of the people, places, and events in these stories have a basis in real life, yet large portions of the tales I've told are entirely fictional. There is a point at which this reality and fiction meet: the search for meaning in life. That search is demanded of us all. We each search in our own way. Some are more successful than others. But search we must. These stories tell of a few such searches, a few attempts to discover a reason for living.

# A
# REASON
# FOR
# LIVING

# *Jocko Coyle*

**M**Y name is John Aloyious Coyle. My friends call me Jocko. My enemies have called me lots of things. That's all right with me—I feel the same way about them. I'm eighty-one years old and still glad to wake up in the morning.

They say a man should try to know himself. For some folks, I'm afraid that'd be a waste of time. A lot of people just aren't worth knowing. In fact, if they ever *did* get to know themselves, it would be pretty frightening. I used to be something like that myself. I believed in "modern" profundities like "moving on toward Progress"—meaning moving on toward moving on. Any African witch doctor would be envious to see all the nonsense modern men accept with such enormous gullibility.

When I was at university in Dublin, I was sure I knew all the answers. Like most young men, I talked a lot about Truth and such. I didn't know what the hell I was talking about. It took me a long time to learn.

"Truth is transcendent reality," Father Malachek used to say. I'd nod wisely, like the rest of the self-important youngsters sitting around me in the lecture hall, but I never really knew what he meant. It took half a century before I finally learned that each of us is part of a reality larger than ourselves. So my professor was right: Truth is never so far from us as we think. Still, most of us usually get bogged down in the details of our lives and lose sight of reality—and Truth—and ourselves. The trick is to remember that we and all the ways we spend (or waste) our time don't constitute the center of the universe. Life is a great gift precisely because it gives us the chance to get outside ourselves and do something for somebody else. So long as we're exclusively interested in getting instead of giving, so long as we insist on trying to be the center of the universe, we miss the point and keep making ourselves unhappy. By the time you're an old goat of eighty-one winters, it's a little easier to see that you and what you do aren't the center of heaven and earth, so it's a little easier to see the reality that's been right there with you all along.

I've had a little more time than most to think about such things. In the fall of 1938, a head-on automobile crash near our little ranch in New Mexico took my dear wife and left me in pretty bad shape. I lost my left eye, my left leg just below the knee, and my left arm at the elbow. We had no insurance and a big mortgage on the ranch, which I lost. It seemed that everything was gone: the growing-up years in Ireland, the move to America, marrying the finest Irish girl that Brooklyn ever produced, the move West to live on the land and build our own place, the years on the ranch, the good life we built—all gone because some bastard from Albuquerque came around a corner on the wrong side of the road.

By the time it was all over, I was a fifty-six-year-old with no wife, no money, no job, no property, and no prospects. I did have one big asset, though: one hell of a fine daughter and a fine son-in-law. I've been with Maggie and Tom ever since.

A man is supposed to teach his children. In the case of Jocko Coyle, I believe my children taught me. Let me tell you a story. . . .

If the shipment of x-ray equipment had arrived on time, the story might be different. Pacific Intermountain Express was running a day late and the new x-ray machine didn't arrive at Spanish Fork until December 23. By then Tom had to work through the night to get the equipment installed in Dr. Sutton's office. It was nearly noon the next day before he left Spanish Fork, heading east across Utah, hurrying toward the Colorado line on Christmas Eve.

The first snow hit the windshield just after Tom left Spanish Fork. The north wind began sweeping the blacktop with swirling patterns of snow. As he headed across Utah at midday, the gray sky reaching eastward to Colorado and the Continental Divide was heavy and forbidding. It was a long drive to Denver even in good weather, but he had to get home. Today was Christmas Eve.

Before he reached the Colorado line, the storm had become a blizzard. Snow was sticking to the wiper blades. Ice was building around the edges of the windows. Even with the heater and defrosters running wide open, he could hardly see the road. The snow-packed road surface was getting slick. Several times he almost lost control on a curve. By the time he had crossed the Colorado line and reached Grand Junction, almost all the traffic had given up and pulled off the road.

When he stopped for gas, a sandwich and a cup of coffee at the truck stop in Grand Junction, the snowfall finally began to taper off. By the time he reached Montrose the snow had stopped, the sky was clearing, and the temperature was dropping fast. The approaching night was going to be clear and cold—very cold.

In Gunnison, he heard that Monarch Pass was un-plowed and almost closed, but he hurried on—tonight was Christmas Eve. As he came closer to the pass over the mountains, the road seemed to become slicker, the air colder. The Hudson was a good automobile which Tom had bought new just a few days before. The trip to Utah was the first time he'd been out of town with the car. In fact, it was so new that he hadn't taken time to get the car insured before he left Denver. He was used to winter driving in the mountains, so he kept going—faster than he should have. He didn't see the cattle truck jack-knifed across the road until he came around the corner. His choice was to hit the truck or hit the ditch. He took the ditch. The Hudson slipped off the road, plowed sideways in a shower of snow, and rolled over twice, landing wheels down in a pasture.

By the time the truckers reached him, he was already getting out of the car, forcing the crumpled door outward, and stepping out to brush off the broken glass. The top of the Hudson was mashed down enough to have broken out the windshield and most of the rest of the windows in the car. Otherwise, the car seemed all right and was still running. With some help from the truckers, he made it back on the road.

The twilight was turning bitter cold and he was still a long way from Denver. Monarch Pass, Trout Creek Pass, South Park, Kenosha Pass, and Turkey Creek Canyon lay ahead, 200 miles of mountain driving in the dead of winter with no glass in the car. He wrapped up as well as he could with all the clothes he could find in the Hudson and started for Denver. It was going to be cold, but what the hell—the kids were home waiting. It was Christmas Eve.

As he came down Monarch Pass, the blast of bitter cold air coming through the smashed windshield filled his eyes with tears which froze as they ran down his cheeks. Tom stopped in Salida at the Elks Club to thaw out. He downed a double shot of whiskey and sipped slowly on a mug of coffee while he shook the ice from his clothes and tried to rub some circulation into his face and hands. One more quick drink and he was back on the road, this time wrapped in an extra blanket he picked up from the bartender.

The trip up the Arkansas Valley and over Trout Creek Pass seemed a little warmer. Either the whiskey and the blanket were helping, or he was getting too cold to feel anything. By the time he reached the Fairplay Hotel in South Park, the dark and the cold were getting to him again. He was having trouble seeing and could hardly move his arms and legs. At the bar in the Fairplay Hotel, his old buddy Doc Oliver warned Tom to stay for the night and go on in the morning. Tom did stay for a couple of drinks and more coffee. He borrowed an oversized horse blanket which he wrapped over the top of everything, wished Doc a Merry Christmas, and headed toward home. Across the rest of South Park, over Kenosha Pass, down through Bailey, over Crow Hill, down Turkey Creek Canyon—Tom kept heading toward home. The cold didn't bother him so much now, but it was getting harder and harder to see. The tears kept filling his eyes and freezing on his face. The sky had cleared with the falling temperature and the moon lit the snow with a cold, ice-blue light. He felt as though he was moving slowly across a world of ice, absolutely alone, unable to feel his hands and feet, driving and driving, yet never making any real progress. The mountains, the snow-laden pines, the ice in the streams, all seemed a part of a frozen world in which he was the only occupant.

Tom was glad to reach the mouth of Turkey Creek Canyon and see the lights of Denver in the distance. By the time he made it home it was after ten o'clock and he was so cold he could hardly move to get out of the car and wade through the snow to his front door.

Maggie stood waiting in the doorway. "Tom, where have you been? We were so worried! Why, you're like ice—let me get you some dry clothes. Danny, get your father a drink." At seven, Danny knew where his dad's whiskey was located in the Thornton household. He also knew his mother well enough to move fast, the first time he was asked.

With a few drinks under his belt and a warm fire before him, Tom began to thaw out. Danny and his mother had already decorated the tree, with a little help from old Jocko. Danny's little brother Frank was asleep upstairs. It was Christmas Eve and Tom Thornton was home.

"Maggie, the Hudson came right through, snow and all. My God, but it was cold with those windows out! By the time I was coming down Turkey Creek, I couldn't feel my hands or feet." Tom ruffled Danny's hair. "At least we're all together for Christmas."

And so we were. The next day dawned clear and cold. Danny and Frank had a big time under the tree. Christmas is always a big time when a boy and his brother are seven and three. Tom and Maggie sat together as we watched the kids and counted the blessings of the Thornton household. The two boys were blessing enough—and the last five years had been good for Tom and Maggie: the x-ray business had grown until Tom was the exclusive H. G. Fisher representative for Colorado, Wyoming, and Utah. The Thorntons weren't rich, but the household had more than enough and the house in Denver was partly paid off. Two years ago, they had even been able to afford bringing me home to live with them after the accident, although I know they would have done that, money or not. Things were looking good for Tom and Maggie.

A week later Tom was in Fitzsimmons Veterans Hospital east of Denver, fighting for his life. What first seemed to be a bad chest cold had quickly become pneumonia. At home in bed, he had been fighting for breath, dying the strangulating death which comes when both lungs are filling with mucous.

Maggie had been trying to get a doctor to the house as Tom got worse. Finally, on the second day, Dr. Neimeyer had come to look at Tom. In an age before antibiotics, such a severe case of pneumonia was usually a death sentence. The doctor started the sulpha drugs and then returned later the same evening. He sat with Tom for a time, listened to his lungs, and then rose to go. As he put on his overcoat, he said to call at any hour if we needed him during the night. Something about the way the doctor spoke left Maggie and me standing there at the door, afraid to look at one another.

By two-thirty the next morning, Tom had awakened, begging for air. We called Dr. Neimeyer and he came. He took one look at Tom and called the fire department. For the next hour, they administered oxygen. By 4 A.M., Tom was on his way to Fitzsimmons Hospital in an ambulance. Maggie, the kids, and I followed in the Hudson. The doctor who checked Tom into Emergency came out a little later to see us in the waiting room. Danny and Frank were sitting on each side of their mother, staring wide-eyed at the doctor as he entered the room. He seemed very tired.

"I'm supposed to write you a letter, but I don't think your husband will last long enough for you to get it. I'm sorry, Mrs. Thornton, we are doing all we can. Frankly, you should prepare yourself for the worst. I don't see how your husband can last much longer."

Uncomprehending, the mother and her young sons stared at the doctor. I stood there leaning on my crutch and hoping that old Jocko was up to doing whatever needed to be done.

That night Tom's fight for survival began in earnest. A man was fighting for his life and a woman was fighting for the survival of her family. Tom Thornton was a bull-necked, barrel-chested Black Irishman, the kind that fought now and asked questions later. With his brash Irish gift of gab, he was a natural salesman and had convinced half the doctors in Colorado, Utah, and Wyoming that H. G. Fisher of Chicago made the best x-ray machines on the market. He was a tough kid who had grown up on Denver's South Side and married the prettiest girl around, Maggie Coyle. Maggie had grown up on our ranch in New Mexico and had gone to Denver to get a job after the Depression hit. From her years on the ranch, she was every bit as tough as her husband. After meeting and marrying in Denver, Maggie and Tom had enjoyed ten good years together.

By the time Tom was in the hospital, he and Maggie were in their mid-thirties and were fiercely proud of their two little Black Irishmen, Danny and Frank. Old Jocko was kind of proud of the whole bunch.

We were out at the hospital every day. Early January

days in Denver are cold enough ordinarily, but riding to the hospital in that Hudson with all the glass knocked out was really cold. Maggie and I would bundle up the boys until their eyes were the only thing showing, then set out across town for Fitzsimmons.

Tom refused to die. Day after endless day we would sit in that waiting room with those damn white neon lights reflecting on the tile floors, talking in hushed tones and pretending to read the newspapers that were scattered over the couches and chairs. Danny and Frank were good little boys, fidgeting no more than normal and not making any real racket. Once in a while one of the doctors would come in and visit a bit with Maggie. There wasn't much to say. Tom was in what they called the kick-off ward, the last stop for the hopeless cases on the way to the graveyard. They had him on oxygen and sulpha drugs, but that was about all they could do.

The trips home were no better. It gets dark early in January and we would make our way home in the Hudson in the bitter cold, with the two kids huddled between us on the front seat. Maggie was no great shakes as a driver, either. Tom had usually done most of the driving. But we made do.

The house was dark and cold when we'd arrive. I'd build up the fire and then help Maggie undress the kids and get them ready for bed. Maggie would kneel down by the bed with Danny and Frank while they said their prayers. "And bless Daddy, God. Please bring him home safe and well."

Maggie was a trooper. After little Danny and Frank were asleep, we'd sit in the kitchen with a cup of coffee. It got so there was nothing left to say. All the optimistic, cheery talk sounded hollow and pointless. Maggie was sitting there with two little kids and an old man with half a body and a crutch.

I suppose it was natural for a woman to pray for help when things were so bad. Probably I'd have prayed too if I thought there was anybody out there listening. Nothing in my life gave me much faith in the whole business. Especially after my wife died, God and I were on the outs. I had the idea that losing her was His fault. But when I'd lie awake at night and think about Maggie and those kids, it started to seem natural to ask for help, if not for Tom's life, at least for whatever it would take for me to help my daughter and her children. When I tried to pray, though, I found I just didn't know how. God and I, if He existed, were still on the outs.

One afternoon we arrived at Fitzsimmons and discovered Tom's bed, made up and empty. Tom was gone! Maggie and I just stood there, fearing the worst, afraid to say so. A nurse came running down the corridor, "Oh, Mrs. Thornton, I was supposed to tell you that your husband has been moved to surgery."

My heart started beating again. Maggie and I took a look at one another and started down the hall.

We met Dr. Grow in the surgical ward. He was a big man, old and grizzled, the kind that came right to the point. "Your husband is somehow still hanging on, but he cannot hope to last much longer unless we find some way to help him. We've got to clear his lungs. We would need your permission to open a large hole in your husband's back. Through that hole we would resect several of his ribs and drain the mucous from his plural cavity. Frankly, he may not be strong enough to survive, but I believe this operation is the only chance he has."

Maggie didn't hesitate a moment. The operation was

scheduled for that afternoon. Maggie and I sat in the waiting room with the kids. Danny and Frank knew something was going on, but didn't ask many questions.

The patients who could get around on their own would come through the waiting room in their slippers and red corduroy robes that said *US Government*. Usually they had a piece of fruit or a candy bar in their pockets for the kids. Danny and Frank would visit with them the way kids will. Nobody said much. We just waited to hear something from Dr. Grow.

It was almost six o'clock that afternoon when he came in from the operating room. It was dark outside and both kids were asleep on the couches. When he came in, Maggie didn't move. She followed the doctor with her eyes as he crossed the room and sat beside her.

"The operation went well. We've started draining his lungs and we're rinsing his plural cavity with a saline solution. That should help dissolve the mucous and give him a chance to breathe. Your husband is a strong man. Frankly, he should already be dead. The fact that he is still alive after the operation and after the past several days is an indication that some inner physical strength or act of will is carrying him through. Please don't get your hopes too high, but I think your husband may have a chance now."

We sat in the waiting room until nearly ten o'clock. Danny and Frank slept. The clock ticked, the neon tubes hummed. Maggie sat just where she was. I watched her, watched the sleeping boys, and thought that God was probably up to His old tricks again—first my wife, now Maggie's husband.

Dr. Grow finally came in again and sent us home. Tom was still unconscious, but his vital signs were stable. The salt water seemed to be flushing out his chest. "I'll be here with him tonight and will call the moment there is any change. Now please get these children home and get some rest yourself."

Old Jocko bestirred his bones. I awakened the children and got Maggie started bundling them up for the ride home. It was after midnight when I watched Maggie kneel by the kids' bed and ask God's help.

The next few days were a blur. We spent so many hours in that waiting room that Danny and Frank were practically adopted by the nurses and those patients in the red robes. Maggie and I waited out the days and nights, talked to Dr. Grow again and again, then waited longer. It was touch and go for almost two weeks. Tom's lungs finally began to clear and stay clear. He regained consciousness and the doctor finally announced that Tom was going to make it.

"Thank you, doctor. You've been wonderful. We owe you Tom's life."

"I don't think so, Mrs. Thornton. I played a part, but your husband did most of the work. He's a fighter. God must have something for him to do, because He simply would not let him die. You must understand that to me, your husband's survival is nothing less than a miracle."

Miracle or not, Tom did survive. We were still back and forth to the hospital every day, but now we were visiting Tom and watching him gradually grow stronger. The pneumonia and the operation had been so devastating that we were told to expect a convalescence of some months before we could bring him home.

I was quite a bit of help with the kids and Maggie. In fact, in those months I began to feel really useful again for the first time since the accident that killed my wife and crippled me. It was then, too, that I first began to know Tom—really know him for the special man he was—or perhaps know him for the special man he had become.

We usually took turns sitting with him. The nurses grew accustomed to seeing Maggie or me visiting most of the day. We had lots of time to talk. It was during one of those visits that I began to see just how much Tom had changed.

Over my wife's objections, I'd raised Maggie with no great love for organized religion. For myself, I'd grown up around the Church and had managed to become pretty skeptical of the whole business. It seemed that most of what passes for organized religion says a lot more about men than about God. Half the world's crimes have been committed by men using religion as a front. When my wife was killed and I was crippled, all the religious gush I heard hadn't made me whole—and it certainly hadn't brought back my dear wife. As near as I could make out, what people call "religion" didn't have much going for it.

Maggie had grown up going through the motions of religious observance for her mother's sake, but was my daughter enough to avoid taking the whole thing too seriously. Tom's upbringing had apparently been about the same. To my thinking, he and Maggie made a fine pair. They both believed in God, but not in the mess men had made in the name of religion. In practice for Maggie and Tom, as for so many people, this usually meant setting God on a back shelf: important, yes—but not really having too much to do with life—sort of a cosmic errand boy. That was all right with me, especially after the accident that killed my wife. I didn't care whether He existed or not.

One February afternoon, I was sitting by Tom's bedside

as the winter sun streamed through the window and re-
flected on the tile floor of the hospital ward. Tom was
propped up on several pillows, staring out the window.
We hadn't said a word in ten minutes. The day before, Dr.
Grow had felt that Tom was strong enough to be moved.
The new bed was in a ward with less traffic. Several
empty beds adjoining our end of the ward were vacant,
giving a very welcome sense of privacy.

Tom was staring out the windows on the southwest end
of the ward. The mountains were a dazzling white in the
early afternoon sun. I'd been sitting there thinking about
the last two months myself. Finally I said, "You were
almost a goner, Tom."

"I *was* gone, Jocko."

I waited. The sun warmed our faces as we looked out
toward the mountains. Finally, Tom spoke again. "For the
first few days—I don't know how long—I kept concen-
trating on trying to imagine Danny and Frank, seeing the
faces of the boys. I kept telling myself I couldn't die
because they had to be raised. They needed me. I couldn't
quit.

"Then one night—I think it was night—I felt someone
enter the room. Didn't open my eyes. I didn't need to.
You can feel Death when it stands by your bed.

"I felt so damn bad it was a kind of relief to know that
things were coming to an end. I don't know how long
Death stood there. I was fighting to breathe—ready to
give up, to make the next heave of my chest the last. Then
I knew that another presence had joined us. I don't know
what happened, but I know that strength was being given
me to go on. I wasn't supposed to quit. There was something I still had to do."

Again Tom paused and stared out at the mountains.

"This was no hallucination, Jocko. To deny what I felt that night would be blasphemy. From that moment on, I had peace, I had strength.

"They say whoever looks for God has found Him. I don't know whether or not I was looking for God. It was more like God was looking for me. Well, He sure found me. When He came I knew I was making a bargain I couldn't break. I knew I wouldn't *ever* be alone again.

"Jocko, I don't know whether I'd been praying or not, but I do know that the one prayer God always seems to answer is a prayer for the strength necessary to do our job. If we have the will to go on—really have the will—God will give us whatever we need."

This was a pretty big load for old Jocko to soak up. For all the reasons I've told you—my reaction to an upbringing in the Church, my "modern education" at university, and, above all, my wife's death—all this talk about God made me a little nervous. God knows, Tom wasn't kidding. He believed every word he said and believed so deeply that he was beyond argument, beyond discussion of any kind. Self-pitying old cynic that I was, I didn't know what the hell to say.

I spent many more afternoons by his bed, but Tom never brought up the subject again. I sure didn't bring it up. Whether I was embarrassed for Tom or for myself I don't know, but I do know I didn't want to hear any more about it.

It was a tough year for the Thornton household. When we brought Tom home from the hospital in April, money was short. We were scrambling to make payments on the house. The private x-ray business had dried up overnight in the spring of 1941 because the government was buying all available production as it stockpiled in readiness for the possibility of war. The doctor told Tom that his chest was such a mess that he could never work again. The doctor didn't say what a man with no money and two small kids was supposed to do if he couldn't work.

Maggie, God bless her, was out hunting for some job, any job, that might help make ends meet. She ran across a chance to pick up a few bucks going door to door soliciting donations of used clothing and furniture for the Salvation Army. Maggie pitched in on that job just the way she did with everything else in her life. She worked hard—and in the process she must have made an impression with her boss. When the opportunity came up to run a Salvation Army store in a farm town north of Denver, they asked Maggie if she and her family could handle it. We jumped at the chance.

By early fall of 1941, we were running a Salvation Army store in Greeley. We had Danny in school. Tom and I watched little Frank and ran the store while Maggie went door to door to solicit donations of old clothes, used appliances, and such to sell in the store. We lived in two rooms above the store. The only way up there was a fire-escape stairway running up the outside of the building on the side facing the alley. Not much, but we made out.

We used one room as a kitchen-dining room, and the other as a combination living room and bedroom. We were in the kitchen cutting up chickens for dinner one Sunday and the kids were listening to the radio in the next room when Danny came running in, "The Japs bombed Pearl Harbor."

"Sure, Danny—now go back in there and listen to the Hartz Mountain Canaries."

"No, no—I'm telling the truth. Come in and listen for yourself."

We did. Sure enough, Danny was right. We were in World War II.

Tom tried to enlist the next day. Tried to ship out with the Navy as a pharmacist's mate because of his x-ray experience. The doctor took one look at Tom's chest x-ray and chewed out the lab technician, grumbling, "I'm too busy for your dumb-ass jokes. Nobody ever lived with a chest like that. Don't bullshit me, that's an x-ray from a cadaver."

Needless to say, Tom was turned down. Back to the Salvation Army. At least that gave me a chance to use my charm on some old gals and get them to part with a quarter to buy one of the plastic purses we had piled on a big table in the middle of the store. Actually, it was kind of fun running the place; we were warm; we weren't hungry; plenty of people were worse off. We could usually scrape up a dime apiece for Danny and Frank to go to the Saturday matinee. That gave them each a nickel for admission and a nickel for popcorn at the Big Chief Theatre across the street from the store.

I rigged up an old tricycle for little Frank and put a bike speedometer on the front wheel. The speedometer was meant for a much larger wheel, so the speed it registered was about ten times as fast as Frank's trike could move. If he went all the way to the back of the store and rode up the center aisle as fast as he could pump, he could just get up to 50 m.p.h. on the speedometer before he hit the front door.

Even though we didn't have much, Maggie was always cheerful. She made do with a little bit, wiped the kids' noses, tucked Danny and little Frank into bed, helped Tom get going again when he felt so bad, and even put up with old Jocko (who I admit wasn't always the easiest man to be around). I *was* generally good to help with a job or tell a story. Anyway, we made do.

We were doing all right, especially considering what a lousy year it had been for Tom. I suppose that's why little Frank wanted to get him a special Christmas present that year. Going on five, he was big enough to walk around the block on his own, so long as he didn't cross the street. The Salvation Army store was right downtown, so his block had its share of stores, including a shoe store that had a big pair of green cowboy boots in the window.

That was over twenty years ago, but I remember those boots like it was yesterday. Frank wanted to get those boots for his dad at Christmas. The fact that he didn't have a dime didn't keep him from dreaming. All told, I suppose he was in that store about a dozen times to check on the price and get a closer look. The old man who ran the little store was always nice. He knew the little boy couldn't buy those boots, but he always talked to him just like he had a real customer.

In those days, Santa did the decorating in our house, so we never set up a tree to get ready for Santa until Christmas Eve. That year the trees were about gone when Frank, Danny, and I went to a Christmas tree lot a couple of blocks from the store. The little, woebegone tree we picked was probably glad to get a home. It seemed like a big deal to the boys and me.

We had another break that Christmas season: we didn't have to go out to do any shopping. We were already sitting in the middle of a mountain of junk. After Christmas dinner, the kids were playing downstairs in the store. Maggie had gone down to check on them, leaving Tom and old Jocko alone with a bottle of whiskey. Since he had come home with us, I had never heard Tom utter another word along the lines of what he had said to me that day when we were alone in the hospital. Old cynic that I was, I was glad he hadn't returned to the subject. It made me nervous. As he stayed silent for so very long, I had a feeling that tonight he was about to start up again. He stared at the brick wall across the alley for a long while and finally spoke.

"Jocko, I didn't tell you the whole story. Sometime after the operation—I don't know when—they were flushing my chest with salt solution. There was a tube running in my back, connected to a jug next to the bed. There was some measuring device which would let in a certain amount of the fluid every time the jug was turned. I guess they were supposed to rotate the jug once during each shift. Don't know what happened for sure. The next thing I knew the jug got flipped over three times in about twenty minutes—once by a nurse, once by an orderly, then by the doctor on the floor. I couldn't talk. I couldn't move. I couldn't even lift my head to tell them. The damn fools were drowning me. My lungs were filling with salt water. And I couldn't move.

"Remember that young army corporal in the bed next to me? He was under military arrest because he tried to kill himself. Shot himself in the head and made a bad job of it. They had him in the hospital to save his life so that they could send him to Leavenworth.

"This guy was in bad shape himself, but he finally realized what was happening. Somehow he made it out of bed, pulled out all the tubes hooked into his body, and got down the corridor to the nurses' station for help.

"He saved my life.

"In the process, I guess he broke loose some of the repairs the doctors had done on his head. They put him back in bed and did what they could. He lasted for a few days, but he never got out of that bed again.

"While he was getting worse, I was getting better. Somehow that kid knew I was on the mend. We even tried to talk a little, not much because we were both in such bad shape. Somehow it seemed important to try.

"At the end, he wanted very much to live. Even when he knew he was going to die, I'm sure he didn't feel like a suicide. He felt he had given his life saving mine.

"Maybe he'd have died anyway. I believe he died for me."

Tom sat staring out the window. He didn't say another word. It was on that Christmas Day that I finally gave in. For the first time I understood Maggie's prayers and Tom's feelings. From that day until now, for over 20 years, I've lived with that understanding.

I was still a long way from convinced about going back to church, but I was back in touch with God. That night I found I could pray again. From that day to this, I've never lost that blessing. From then on I stopped feeling sorry for myself—at least I started counting my blessings. Now I can pray, pray to a God Who not only exists, but Who knows that Old Jocko exists.

Strange reason for a conversion? Not really. God's always there when we finally look around and see the real world. He's been waiting for us all the time.

That's the lesson I learned from my children.

# A Job to Be Done

THE big mountains had been threatening snow since early morning. By mid-afternoon the sky to the west had turned black. The first heavy flakes of the April snow were sticking to the pavement in downtown Denver. Walking up 15th Street toward the City and County Building, the two men hunched more deeply into their overcoats.

The taller of the two turned to his short, stocky companion, "I don't think this winter will ever end. My God, Jimmy, it's been snowing for six months. I haven't been *really* warm since last summer."

"To hear you tell it, Billy, you haven't been warm in twenty years," Jimmy laughed. His long, lanky, rail-thin partner had been complaining about the cold ever since they were kids together on the south side of Denver.

It was late April 1925, and the two Treasury agents were on their way to a meeting with the head of the Alcohol and Tax Division, their immediate superior in the Denver office.

Billy grunted and turned up his collar, "You'd better quit worrying about whether or not I'm cold and start worrying about what you're going to tell Tom Morris when we get to his office. When Connie called she said he was sore as hell. Last night's raid really stirred things up."

"I can't help it if Morris is afraid of his shadow. Every time the police department in this town says jump, Morris wants to know how high."

"Maybe so, but we're still going to catch hell for last night," Billy sighed.

By the time the two men arrived at the City and County Building, the spring snowstorm was so heavy that they could hardly see the gold dome of the state capitol across the street. The large, soft flakes sticking to their hats and coats gave them the look of snowmen, one short and stocky, one tall and thin.

"You sure took your time getting here." The dark-haired young secretary in the outer office of the Treasury wing shook her head. "The boss has been chewing the wallpaper since about ten o'clock this morning, ever since the police report came in on last night's raid. Chief Tanner's been on the phone every hour on the hour, all day. I think Mr. Morris is going to kill the two of you."

"Now Connie, my dear, don't fret," Jimmy grinned as he slapped the snow from his hat and coat. "You're far too pretty for that. Besides, Morris will be all right."

Billy looked up and said, "I'm glad to hear Morris will be all right. That being the case, I think I'll just mosey along and let you talk to him."

The door to the inner office opened. A red-faced Tom Morris charged out in his shirt sleeves, snarling, "You mosey your asses into my office—and don't worry about having to talk. I'll do all the talking. All you lard-heads have to do is listen. Not that you ever pay attention to anything you're told!"

The Treasury boss could hardly wait for the office door

to close. He lit into Billy and Jimmy as they came into the room. "Tanner's been on the phone all day. What are you bastards trying to do, fix it so I lose my pension? What did you do last night, anyway? This time you've gone too far. Tanner wants your heads on a plate—and by God, I think I'll let him have your asses this time. I'm tired of taking the heat for the two of you."

Billy and Jimmy knew from experience that the only way to handle their boss was to wait for him to run down. This time it took about ten minutes. Finally Morris was silent. The balding, paunchy, florid little man sat back in his chair and chewed his unlit cigar while he rubbed the desk top with his sweating hands.

Jimmy finally spoke. "Tom, you know as well as I do that Tanner and half the cops on the Denver force are on the take. Of course they yell when we hit their bootlegger buddies hard. Last night we got 'em good. What do you expect Tanner to do, give you a kiss?"

Morris had been mad all day. Now he was just tired. "Damn it, Jimmy, you know I've got to have something solid. You keep giving me some two-bit police sergeant on the take and then tell me he's part of a conspiracy involving the chief of police, the mayor, and every other big shot in town. Why stop there? Why not a senator or two, or maybe the President? Cripes, you guys make me sick!"

Jimmy leaned forward in his chair. "If you keep telegraphing all our punches, letting them know what we're doing, apologizing in advance to Tanner and his cronies, how in hell do you expect us to pin those guys down?"

"Jimmy, we've got to cooperate with the other law enforcement agencies." Morris was sounding plaintive now. "We don't have anywhere near enough people to do this job alone. If we jailed all the people who were drinking or selling alcohol, everybody in this town would be in jail, including the three of us. Meanwhile you guys don't bother with search warrants, you don't care who you throw in the can, whose property you bust up, who you accuse—how the hell do you expect me to defend you?"

"How do you expect us to enforce the law and deal with lice like Tanner when you don't back us?" Jimmy shouted. "When half the cops and judges and prominent bigwigs in town are a part of the system, what do you expect us to do?"

Tom Morris sighed and looked out the window as the snow fell into a darkening twilight. "I keep hearing all this talk about Tanner and his bad cops, but I sure don't see any hard evidence. I'll tell you this: You keep up all the wild charges and half-assed raids that don't prove those charges and you'll get such a mess going that I'll have to choose between saving my tail or saving the two of you. Guess what I'll choose then, geniuses! Now get out of here and stop causing so damn much trouble."

As Jimmy started to open his mouth, Morris stood up, leaning over the desk, "Goddamn it, I mean it. Now get out, both of you!"

On the way through the outer office, Connie flashed Jimmy a knowing grin. "Mr. Morris will be all right, will he? Boy, you sure handled him, Jimmy!"

"Look, beautiful, you should learn not to eavesdrop."

"Eavesdrop?" she replied. "Everybody in this building heard that shouting match."

Jimmy pulled on his overcoat and picked his hat off the rack. As he creased the hat with the side of his hand, he turned to the girl and asked, "Now that you're through with your excitement for the day, how about dinner?"

"The last time I had dinner with you, I got left halfway

through because some stoolie brought you a hot tip you had to check out right away."

"Not tonight, baby, word of honor. I'll take you to Boggio's. Come on, give me a break. This has been a hard day and I need some time with the prettiest girl in town. Billy, why don't you call Sue and bring her to dinner, too?"

Morris' door flew open again. He stood there in his striped shirt and suspenders, his face a bright crimson. "It's not enough that you ruin my life and embarrass the United States Treasury; no, you've got to celebrate! Where do you celebrate? At the fanciest speakeasy in town. I can see the headline now: Treasury agents enjoy an evening on the town at Boggio's, popular local speakeasy! Now, if you troublemakers are through filling your social calendar, why don't you get out and stay out. And as for you, Connie, you keep running around with these bums and you'll probably wind up in jail."

\* \* \*

Nate Boggio was a short, enormously fat man. His jowls and bald head glistened with sweat as he made his way among the customers at the bar and at the tables scattered over the room. In his dark pin-stripe suit with its inevitable white carnation, Nate was always visible, always glad-handing. He had a reputation for good liquor, good food, and stiff prices. His unofficial motto was "It may cost an arm and a leg, but nobody ever got poisoned in my joint."

The snow had stopped at dark. By nine o'clock the evening crowd was out on the town and Boggio's was full. Jimmy and Billy were sitting at a table in a corner, waiting for Connie and Sue to return from the powder room.

They were already one drink ahead of the girls and had just ordered another round.

"Here they come now," Billy said as the girls appeared. The girls were the same Mutt and Jeff pair as Billy and Jimmy. Sue was light-skinned, tall, and skinny, a perfect match for Billy. Connie was short, dark, and a pretty girl by anyone's standard. The four had been spending a lot of time together for the last few months.

Just after the girls were seated at the table, the waiter arrived with the next round of drinks. "The gentleman at the bar sends his compliments. He paid for the drinks and sent this note."

"Which gentleman?" Jimmy asked as he took the note.

"He's right over there," the waiter replied. "No, wait a minute, he must have left for a moment—he's not there now."

"Well, let's see what the mystery man has to say." Jimmy opened the note. His face clouded over as he read.

"What's the matter, honey?" Connie asked.

"Nothing, just some wise guy. C'mon, let's have a good time. Drink your drink."

More drinks and dinner followed. A little after eleven, Connie raised her glass and announced to the table, "Well, we've got to give you two credit for once, we actually made it through dinner without your doing a disappearing act."

"How are my friends, tonight?" Nate Boggio stood by the table with the ever-present glass of red wine in his hand.

"Hello, Nate. Nice dinner tonight."

"Glad you liked it, Jimmy. Now I got something special to give you for dessert—a piece of advice. If you're smart, you'll watch it pretty close when you get up to leave. I don't know who you've been botherin' lately, but the word's out. Somebody's mad enough to hurt you bad if they get a chance."

Billy looked around the room. "Who is it?"

Nate Boggio smiled that Mona Lisa smile of his. "Hey, I'm just a friend of man. People don't tell me stuff like that. I just know what I hear—and what I hear isn't healthy for you guys. Besides, if there's any shooting around here, it's bad for business. All I know for sure is somebody wants you dead." Boggio moved away across the room.

"Hell," Jimmy muttered, "in this town you can't tell whether the hoods or the cops are after you."

"What was in that note, Jimmy?" Billy asked.

"Just about what Nate said. Our mysterious friend at the bar was concerned about our health, too. Anyway, I guess we'd better pay attention. You gals go home on your own." Jimmy rose. "I'll call a cab."

"Oh Billy," Sue reached out to touch his arm, "will you be all right?"

Connie snapped her purse shut. "I knew it was too good to last. We never get through a whole evening without something like this!"

"Here's a few bucks for the cab. I'll call you tomorrow," Jimmy said. "Billy and I will be fine. We'll stay here a few more minutes and then head home ourselves."

The girls went out to the street alone, leaving Jimmy and Billy sitting at the table. Crowded and noisy, Boggio's was heating up for the evening.

"Now what?" asked Billy.

"Let's sit here for a while," Jimmy replied. "This is probably just a false alarm anyway. If there is somebody out there, it's probably because of last night's raid. I wonder, is this the bootleggers? Or maybe we finally made Chief Tanner and the boys so mad that they'll try something really stupid."

Billy played with a packet of matches. "Wish we knew who wrote that note. Boggio doesn't want trouble in here. I understood his position. At least I think I do. But what was the other guy's angle?"

Jimmy shifted his shoulder holster. "Well, let's go find out."

The street outside was cold and wet. The melting snow gave off a rising fog that left the street dark and shadowed. The street lights and the lights of the cars glowed through the mist. The car was parked on a side-street around the corner from Boggio's. As they walked around the corner to where they had parked, not a soul was in sight.

Billy looked at the dark street behind him. "If somebody was going to take a shot at us, they've already had a good chance. Maybe we'd better take a good look at the car. Somebody may have left us a little surprise."

Jimmy raised the hood and found what they were afraid they'd find. Three sticks of dynamite were taped to the fire wall, with one wire running to the battery and another to the ignition. "My God, if we'd started that car we'd have been scattered all over town!"

They very carefully disconnected the wires and removed the dynamite. As Jimmy and Billy drove across town to the apartment they shared in South Denver, they went over the events of the evening. Jimmy mused, "I wonder how so many people found out about this—Boggio—our mysterious note writer—who else? Maybe we were supposed to find that bomb. Maybe they didn't want to blow us up. Maybe somebody just wanted to scare us."

"Well then, whoever it was sure did a good job of that!" Billy eyed the dynamite on the seat of the car.

"Tomorrow let's nose around and see who knows what." Jimmy lit a cigarette. "Maybe somebody wanted to scare us off without causing any heat. Killing Treasury agents makes a lot of people nervous."

"Yeah," Billy sighed, "me for one."

\* \* \*

Tom Morris looked around his office at the six agents and thought, "Six—for God's sake—six kids in their twenties and thirties to control this whole town—most of the state, for that matter! No wonder we can't do anything about Prohibition."

Word had travelled fast. By early morning Morris knew about last night's bomb. "I'm not much for meetings, but I thought it was about time to regroup before all you rum-dums got yourselves killed."

Jimmy and Billy were there—the last to arrive, as usual. Paul Nodacker and Jolly Prance were the oldest team of agents. Paul was a big man, sullen and silent. He was an exact opposite of little Jolly, the rosy-cheeked, enthusiastic clown who always had a new joke, usually at his own expense. The four of them had been working for Treasury in Denver for almost a year. The other two men were new and had just been reassigned to Denver from Kansas City.

Morris took the cigar from his mouth, "What can you tell me about the bomb?"

Jimmy shrugged. "It didn't go off."

Morris flushed. "Smart asses, nothing but smart asses. What do you think this is, some kind of a game? Look, let's get one thing straight. All the cowboy antics are over.

From now on we do everything by the book—*by the book!* Do you understand? We cooperate with local law enforcement and we coordinate *everything* we do through this office."

Morris spent the balance of the meeting outlining his plans for the month, reading aloud from the Washington directives, stressing the importance of written reports. Then he ran them out of his office. On the way out, Connie stopped Jimmy and Billy. "What really happened last night?"

Jimmy smiled. "Nothing really, just a false alarm."

Connie didn't smile. "If he won't take care of himself, will you please take care of him, Billy?"

Back on the street the partners looked at one another. "You know, Billy, I still don't think somebody was trying to kill us. If you were going to take somebody out, would you tell the whole town first? No, somebody was trying to scare us. Maybe we're closer than we thought. Maybe we're making Tanner nervous."

"Jimmy, will you forget Tanner? We're in enough trouble. Can't you just do your job?"

"Billy, that *is* our job. We'll keep busting two-bit bootleggers and *never* change anything until we get Tanner and the whole bunch behind him."

"What if you're wrong, Jimmy?" Billy knew there was no use asking that question. In all the years he had known Jimmy Carr, the thought that he might be wrong had never entered the cocky little Irishman's mind.

As Billy started their car, a large presence leaned in the open window on the driver's side. "Hear you guys almost blew up last night. Better be careful." The voice belonged to Tom Leahy, a lieutenant on the Denver Police Force.

"Disappointed, Leahy?" Jimmy bristled.

"You'll just never learn, will you, Jimmy? You never could tell your friends from your enemies," Leahy shook his head.

"You work for Tanner, that's good enough for me," Jimmy bristled.

"Remember, I told you: Be careful." Leahy was gone.

Billy sat for a moment. "Was that a threat or is the guy really worried about us? I'm getting so I can't tell who's on our side and who's out to get us."

"Let's go see Tanner. I'm tired of talking to his stooges," Jimmy replied. "He'll be eating lunch at Saliman's."

Saliman's was an old saloon near Larimer Street, a holdover from the free lunch days before the turn of the century. The steam tables were still in place and, although the signs outside no longer advertised alcohol for sale, you didn't need to know anybody special to get a drink inside. The old mosaic tile floor, the ancient bar, the waiters in the white aprons—not much had changed.

Jimmy was right: There sat Chief of Police Rugg Tanner. Tall, heavy-set, florid, sporting a great thatch of unruly white hair, Tanner was easy to locate. He was a familiar face all over Denver. In an age when many men on both sides of the law let hired stooges do their fighting for them, Tanner had a reputation as a man who liked to do his own fighting.

As they came up to the table, one of the detectives sitting with Tanner started to stand up. Jimmy pressed down hard on his shoulder and kept him from rising. As the detective started to twist out of Jimmy's grasp, his right hand reached for the gun in his shoulder holster.

Tanner spoke sharply, "Hold it! Put that piece away." The detective hesitated for just a second—and then slumped back into his seat, red-faced and muttering.

"Well, look who's here," Tanner said in his deep voice. "If it isn't Jimmy Carr and Billy Bonnie. I heard you guys were laying low after that little deal at Boggio's last night. You know, I was worried about you. You really ought to be more careful."

"What's the matter, Tanner, are we getting too close?" Jimmy growled through clenched teeth.

"Always ready to fight, aren't you kid?" Tanner shook his head. "Trouble is, you usually fight the wrong people. You never seem to know who your friends are."

"That's the second time today somebody's told me that."

"Well, they're right, kid. Take me, for example. It would be a lot easier for me to help you if you didn't keep telling everybody about all my imaginary connections with the bootleggers. As long as you think the whole police force is in the tank, how can you expect us to help you?"

"I don't want any help from you or your coppers, Tanner. Your hands are too dirty for me. We just came here to tell you that we don't scare so easy as you think. Play those games with the bomb threats as much as you want. We're going to keep at it until we see you in jail. And tell your flat foot friend here that if he ever tries to pull a gun on me again I'll shoot his fat ass."

Tanner went pale and his knuckles tightened on his chair, but he didn't rise. "Okay, kid, have it your way."

Billy and Jimmy half walked and half backed to the door of the saloon. As they stepped into the street, Billy grabbed his partner. "Jesus, now I know you're crazy! Are you trying to get us killed? What the hell do you think you're doing?"

34

"Take it easy and keep walking. Don't you get it? Tanner doesn't like being pushed, so we're going to push him harder. We'll push him until he does something stupid. And he will, Billy, he will."

Billy muttered, "I sure hope we're here to see it."

* * *

"Billy, your mother's right. Everything that you and Jimmy are doing is just too dangerous. You can't go on this way!"

The anguish showed plainly on Sue's long, thin face as she spoke. She knew that the friendship between Billy and Jimmy was too close for any criticism. She knew that she threatened her own relationship with Billy by even bringing up the matter. But being here in Mrs. Bonnie's home, hearing the widow tell her son that his job as a prohibition agent had become too dangerous, had brought Sue's own fears to the surface. She loved Billy and didn't want to lose him.

Billy had been getting hit from both sides ever since he and Sue arrived at his mother's house for dinner. He was angry with his mother for involving Sue in a family row, and even more angry because Mrs. Bonnie had chosen to invite Father Horrigan, the family's parish priest, to be on hand as well. Billy was reacting to the pressure by ducking his head lower and lower, flushing more deeply, and saying less and less.

"Since your father died, you're all I have. Billy, it's not fair to risk your life in this job. It's not fair to me and it's not fair to Susan."

Father Horrigan waited in the overheated, overfurnished parlor of the little house in South Denver, waited for Mrs. Bonnie and Sue to express all the fears which poured from them, waited in vain for Billy to rise to his own defense.

Finally, the tall, angular, red-faced, old priest with the close-cropped white hair lit his pipe and shook out the match, leaning forward to drop the match in the ashtray sitting before him on the table. "Now, Rose, give the boy a chance. He knows you're concerned. He loves you and he loves Susan. But no amount of tears will wash away his loyalty to Jimmy Carr. The two of them have been friends since they were little shavers.

"And remember something else, Rose. Billy's a man now, a man who has chosen to take on a job. You have no business pushing him to quit that job. If he decides to quit, or to leave Jimmy on his own, that's his decision. But if you women take over Billy's life and do his deciding for him, about his friendship with Jimmy, or this job, or anything else for that matter, then you, and Susan, and Billy, are all the losers."

"Dear God, Father! I bring you into my home as Billy's spiritual adviser and ask that you help him back to right reason—and *this* is what you give me! Aloyious Horrigan, you know what I ask is reasonable. How can you say such things to my son?"

The old priest's face was always red. Now it was a bright crimson. "Rose Bonnie, what you want of Billy may be reasonable to you, but I ask you to remember that the reason of man and the reason of God are two very different things!"

Mrs. Bonnie rose from her chair, trembling. She spoke very slowly as she looked directly at the priest. "So now your opinions are the reason of God. If I hadn't known you for these last thirty years, I would never have believed that a priest of Mother Church could ever be such a wrong-headed meddler!"

"Called or not, God is always present. He's here with us now, Rose, and He knows that Billy must make up his own mind and carry out his own responsibilities. If you and Susan love Billy as much as you say, you already know that.

"And as for you, Billy. This is your decision. Make it like a man. If you wait 'til everyone is happy with what you decide, I can tell you one thing—*you* won't be happy with the decision."

The angular old priest rose to go. "I've said my piece tonight, Rose, and I'll not apologize for that. I know you're mad at me for telling you the truth and I will do one thing to make up for it. I'll speak to Jimmy Carr. He always was hell-bent for having his own way and fighting the whole world. He was that way the first day I saw him in the orphanage and I've never seen him any other way.

"I still think the boys must decide for themselves, but I will have a talk with Jimmy and ask him to slow down a bit. Now good night to you all."

Billy, his mother and his girl watched silently as Father Horrigan put on his coat, stepped out the front door of the little house, and closed the door behind him.

\* \* \*

Jimmy Carr and Father Horrigan sat across from one another in the corner booth of a small roadhouse nestled in the foothills west of Denver. They had driven out on Morrison Road at Father Horrigan's urging.

"I won't take up much of your time, Jimmy, but I do need to talk to you." The priest paused to light his pipe while the barmaid put two glasses of beer on the table.

Jimmy sat absolutely still, eyeing the priest, and waiting for him to continue.

"Jimmy, they say the British Isles are made up of four nations—the Scots who keep the Sabbath and anything else they can lay hands on; the Welsh who pray on their knees and on their neighbors; the English who consider themselves a race of self-made men, thereby relieving the Almighty of a terrible responsibility; and the Irish, who don't know what the devil they want and are willing to fight anyone for it. I know you're willing to fight, Jimmy, but what the devil *do* you want?"

Jimmy shifted in his seat. "Father, what the devil do *you* want? I don't know what you're talking about!"

"I'm talking about the job you and Billy have with the Treasury Department. The way things have been going lately, you've scared Mrs. Bonnie and Susan out of their wits."

"Billy, too?"

"You know better than that, Jimmy. Billy will stick with you no matter what. What I want to know is what's so important about this job. Why risk your life or your friend's life?"

Jimmy drank half his beer in one long draught. "I'm not going to let those bastards put the run on me."

Father Horrigan shook his head. "Same old Jimmy—it doesn't matter whom you fight as long as you fight. Tell me the truth now, what's the sense in that? Do you have some special license to scare the hell out of everybody? Do you think God cares one way or the other?"

Jimmy moved convulsively and almost stood up in the booth. "I figured God would get into this conversation pretty soon. What does God have to do with it? Why do you always drag God into everything?"

Father Horrigan put his pipe on the table and leaned forward. "Don't use me as an excuse, Jimmy. God is here now—waiting. He's always with us. He's not my creation. You and I are *His* creation."

Jimmy leaned forward to confront the priest. "What a man does is up to him, not up to your God."

"Don't give me all that bull about being a man, as though that somehow replaced God. You can't replace God by talking about man, no matter how loud your voice."

"You never change, do you Father? You've been spouting that guff ever since I first saw you when I was a little kid. You and that God of yours—you're always talking about Him or to Him!"

"Jimmy, if we talk to ourselves as though God weren't there, we're talking to the Devil. You can't really *be* a man unless you let God into your life."

Jimmy Carr rose to go and then turned back to face the old priest. "I *am* a man and I don't need to kowtow to you or your God to know how a man acts. I thought you wanted to talk to me—you didn't. All this was just another excuse to preach. Well, I don't want to listen to that anymore!"

Jimmy went out the door, leaving the old priest sitting at the table. Father Horrigan finished his beer, shook his head, and murmured, "Still the tough guy who can do it all. Jimmy, you have a lot to learn. I hope the price of that lesson isn't too high when the time comes to pay the bill."

\* \* \*

The night was clean and cold. As the car climbed the switch-backs on the face of Lookout Mountain, the lights of Denver lit the valley floor below, stretching away to the east. Connie and Jimmy were on the way to a roadhouse on the top of the Front Range, out for dinner and dancing. On the drive from town, Connie had returned to one of her frequent themes: Jimmy's return to law school.

"Jimmy, you have two years under your belt, you tell me you love the law, Dean Scheer says you're the best student he's ever had in his class at Westminister—why not go back and finish? You took this Treasury job because they were hiring people with law school training at a time when you needed the money. We've got enough money now to finish. I could keep working. Finish while you have a chance."

Jimmy snapped, "Well, I'll be damned! First, it's Mrs. Bonnie and Sue, then it's Horrigan—now you. I'm not going to quit, not for you, not for anybody."

"Jimmy, what's so important about this job? You know how dangerous the whole thing has become. Now is the time to get out. Won't you please at least think about it?"

Jimmy stared straight ahead as he drove, "I'm not going to quit until Rugg Tanner's in jail where he belongs."

Connie was on the verge of tears. "It's not Rugg Tanner, it's not bootleggers, it's your damned insistence on being a tough guy. I know you're tough, Jimmy! We all do. Don't die just to prove how tough you were. I need you alive—I need you!"

Neither of them said another word as they drove through the clear, cold moonlit night. The frost on the pine trees glistened in the headlights as they wound along the narrow mountain road. Ahead the lights of the roadhouse gleamed through the darkness.

"I've never been up here, but I hear it's a good place." Jimmy turned to Connie as the car stopped. "Come on, kid, let's forget this for tonight and have a good time."

"I'd have a better time if I knew you were going back to law school."

"Connie, I am going back to law school, as soon as I finish this Treasury job. I want to be a lawyer. Dean Scheer is right—I'll be a good lawyer. But first I'm going to finish what I've started. Now let's have a good time tonight."

The roadhouse was unusually quiet, even for a week night. Most of the tables were empty and there were only two other couples on the dance floor. "Maybe it's early yet. Let's have a drink, Connie, and wait for things to liven up."

Several drinks came and went, but the place remained quiet. Connie and Jimmy were alone on the dance floor. One of the other couples had left and the remaining man and woman were paying their bill and apparently preparing to leave. The bartender visited quietly with one man at a corner of the bar while two others shot pool at a table in the rear of the roadhouse. Outside the crunch of gravel announced the arrival of another car in the parking lot. A moment later, three men entered the roadhouse and went straight to the bar, joining the group in the back of the room. One of the men stopped shooting pool and began to turn out the lights over several tables along the far side of the room.

Connie felt Jimmy grow tense as they danced to the music from the juke box. "Are you getting hungry, Jimmy?"

"Forget dinner!" Jimmy whispered. "This is a setup. I know one of the hoods who just came in. Somebody's recognized me and they're planning a little party."

As Jimmy whispered to Connie, the remaining couple settled their bill with the bartender and stepped out into the night. Jimmy held Connie close as they danced, speaking softly in her ear. "We're in trouble now. They'll be making a move soon. Just keep dancing. Smile. I'll move us gradually toward the door. Damn it, I said smile! And when I say run, sprint for the car. Don't look back. Just get to the car as quickly as possible. When you're inside, duck down on the seat. Don't put up your head for anything."

Connie held him tight as they danced. "Oh, Jimmy. What about my purse?"

"Forget the purse. We're almost to the door. When I say go, run like hell! Now!"

Connie stepped through the door into the night air and ran across the gravel toward Jimmy's car. Jimmy raced beside her, half dragging her by the arm as he reached for his keys. She dove into the seat as he started the car. As the Model T roared to life, shots rang out from the roadhouse door. The windshield shattered, spraying glass across Connie as she crouched down on the seat. As the car turned onto the road in a spray of gravel, two more shots struck the car.

Coming down Lookout Mountain with the cold mountain air rushing through the jagged edges of the broken windshield, Jimmy watched the mirror closely for signs of pursuit. No one came. Connie sat in the broken glass, wrapped up against the cold of the night air. At first she was silent, then she turned to Jimmy and began to cry. "Please hold me. Stop the car and hold me."

The ride home afterward was long and cold. When they reached South Denver, Connie sat for a moment before going into her house. "Jimmy, I don't know how much more of this I can handle. I love you. But I don't know how much more I can handle."

* * *

Had the call come ten minutes earlier, Billy and Jimmy would have been there to receive the tip. That ten minutes changed everything: Billy and Jimmy had left for Limon, a town in eastern Colorado with reports of a new source of bootleg whiskey; instead, Jolly Prance and Paul Nodacker happened to be in the Treasury office when the caller left the tip.

"If you want real proof on Rugg Tanner, get up to Idaho Springs. Tanner's bookkeeper is in the office at the Argo Tunnel. He'll be looking for you tonight. Be there by eleven if you want Tanner's private set of books. Don't be late."

Connie started to ask for a name, but the caller hung up.

"What was it, Connie?" Jolly Prance asked.

"An anonymous tip—supposed to be Rugg Tanner's bookkeeper. The message was for Jimmy Carr. I don't know what to do. Billy and Jimmy are heading east to Limon. It's after four now. They won't reach Limon 'til about seven. Even if I could get hold of them, there's no way they could get back in Denver and all the way up to Idaho Springs by eleven. Jimmy will really be mad he missed the tip. What can I do?" Connie looked at Jolly and his hulking, sullen partner, Paul Nodacker.

Nodacker spoke up. "It's probably a phony, anyway. The Argo Tunnel's been closed for years. Why drive way up in the mountains on a wild goose chase like this?"

"I don't know," Jolly responded. "It might be a wild goose chase. On the other hand, this might be the break we've been looking for. Imagine, Tanner's books!"

43

Paul bristled, "I say we don't go!"

Jolly grinned, "I say we do. You stay here if you don't want to come. I'm going to Idaho Springs and take a look."

"All right," Paul grunted. "Let's go. Could we at least stop for something to eat on the way up there? No sense wasting the whole evening."

Little Jolly grinned from ear to ear as the two men went out the door. "Connie, tell Jimmy we went to get the proof he wants on Tanner!"

The late afternoon sun was in their eyes as Jolly and Paul's car wound its way up Clear Creek Canyon. They arrived in Idaho Springs in plenty of time for dinner, eating in the hotel on the main street. During dinner, Paul argued against the meeting. "I don't see why you're so all-fired hot to go up to the Argo Tunnel office. The place is boarded up. Hell, this might be a trap. What do you want to do, get us killed, Jolly?"

"Paul, we're already here. Now let's go take a look. You watch my back and I'll watch yours. Now let's go."

High on the mountain side overlooking Idaho Springs, the Argo Tunnel was a relic of Colorado's mining heyday. The office which enclosed the south end of the tunnel had been boarded up for years. As Paul and Jolly drove up the hill, they saw no light, no sign of life. Paul Nodacker twisted uneasily in the car seat. "For God's sake, Jolly, don't go in there!"

Jolly lifted his automatic from his shoulder holster. "We're here, now let's take a look."

Nodacker was about fifteen feet behind as Jolly reached the door of the Argo Tunnel office. The door stood slightly ajar. As Jolly reached the threshold, a double barreled sawed-off shotgun fired point blank from inside

44

the building. Jolly was lifted off his feet and hurled backward by the blast. He never knew what hit him.

As Nodacker raced back down the hill to the car, he shouted, "It's me, Paul. Don't shoot, for God's sake!" In a moment he was back in the car and on his way down the hill to Idaho Springs.

\* \* \*

Six men stared at the early morning light as it streamed into the Treasury Department offices, leaving paths of blue light as it sliced through the cigar smoke. Paul Nodacker had just finished telling his story.

Jimmy Carr spoke up. "Nodacker, how come you're here and Jolly's dead?"

Nodacker bristled, "Goddamn it, I told you once. When Jolly went down, I rushed inside the tunnel office. I heard a noise in the back and fired a couple of shots toward the sound. Whoever it was must have ducked out the back. I didn't see or hear another damn thing."

"If this guy with the shotgun was shooting people, why didn't he shoot you, too?"

"I guess he scared off. How the hell do I know!" Nodacker stood up and faced Jimmy. "If you've got so damn many questions, why don't you ask the guy that shot Jolly?"

Jimmy stood and looked up at Nodacker. "I'm going to do exactly that, you chickenshit bastard. And if I find that you ran out on Jolly, I'll shoot you myself!"

"That's enough!" Tom Morris rose behind his desk. "Everybody sit down and shut up! We're going to do something about this, but we're going to do it my way. Those bastards are going to pay for Jolly. We'll give them a raid they'll never forget. Half the hoods and half the booze in this town are in the Denargo Market. We're going to raid them and shut 'em down for good."

"Who's going to do that—the six of us?" Billy raised an eyebrow. The two new agents from the Kansas City office exchanged glances. Billy continued, "Hell, there's enough artillery in Denargo to start a war!"

Morris chewed his unlit cigar. "I've already thought of that. Wired Cheyenne an hour ago. Six agents are driving down for the raid. They'll be here this afternoon. We'll hit the Denargo Market tonight."

After the morning meeting, the day moved slowly. The agents hung around the office, recleaned an arsenal of handguns, shotguns, machine guns. By early afternoon they had gone their separate ways, agreeing to meet at the Treasury office at ten that evening.

It was after nine when Jimmy and Billy parked behind the City and County Building and started to walk inside to the Treasury offices. A large figure stepped out of the shadows as they approached the door. Jimmy and Billy both reached for their shoulder holsters.

"Take it easy!" It was Leahy, the police lieutenant. "Step back in the shadows. We need to visit."

"Still running errands for Tanner, I see," Jimmy snarled.

"Think whatever you damn please, but you better listen and *listen good!* I don't have much time. I shouldn't be here at all. Don't raid Denargo Market tonight. They know you're coming and it's a setup. The booze is gone. The hoods are gone. The newspaper boys are going to be there and put the laugh on twelve T-men who bust in on a bunch of vegetable stands."

"How do you know about the raid?" Billy asked. "Nobody knew except the agents in the Treasury office!"

"Yeah, that's right," Leahy replied. "Maybe you'd better keep an eye on your own people. Meanwhile, you'd better kill that raid or you guys are going to look really bad. The newspapers will run you guys out of town.

"And one more thing—the deal in Idaho Springs. That wasn't meant for Jolly Prance. It was meant for the two of you." Leahy turned and was gone as quickly as he had come.

Upstairs in the Treasury offices ten men waited for the time to move. As Jimmy and Billy came in the door, Tom Morris half rose behind his desk.

"Can I see you for a minute, Tom?" Jimmy asked.

"Can't it keep?"

"No, it can't."

"Okay, let's go outside."

In the outer office, Tom Morris and Jimmy faced each other. "Okay, Jimmy, what is it?"

"Tom, we've got a stoolie. The Denargo Market raid has been tipped off. They're ready to make fools of us."

"How could that be—only the six of us knew!"

"Yeah, only the six of us knew." Jimmy shifted his weight from side to side. And one of 'em was that son of a bitch Nodacker, who didn't get a scratch on him while Jolly was being gunned down."

"You can't prove that!"

"The hell I can't. You give me half an hour with Nodacker and he'll be glad to tell you himself."

Morris was silent for thirty seconds, chewing his dead cigar. "Okay, Jimmy, I'll give you this one. But if it goes sour, you're on your own. I don't know anything about it."

The two men returned to the inner office. Morris spoke first. "Okay, boys, the raid's off. Never mind why. I said the raid's off. Good night."

As Nodacker walked out the door to the parking lot behind the building, Jimmy caught up and tapped him on the shoulder. "How about a drink, Nodacker? It's been a hard day."

"I don't want a drink. What did you say to Morris? Why did he stop the raid?"

"I think you know the answer, Nodacker. It seems some of your friends found out about the raid. Some of those same friends that killed Jolly, you lousy son of a bitch!"

Nodacker stepped away from Jimmy, reaching for his shoulder holster as he moved. Jimmy reached for his automatic and dove to the side as Nodacker fired. The first bullet sprayed bits of asphalt in Jimmy's face. A second tore through his left shoulder. Jimmy fired twice and Nodacker crumpled to the pavement. He was dead before he hit the ground.

\* \* \*

Jimmy had been in St. Luke's Hospital for two days. His left arm was still in a sling, but the doctors had promised to discharge him today. He was already dressed, fidgeting around the room, waiting for the discharge orders, when Tom Morris came in.

"Jimmy, I've got to talk to you. The newspaper boys are ready to climb all over you on this Nodacker thing. I've had one hell of a time keeping the story out of the papers this long."

"What's so bad that we have to hide? I killed Nodacker in self-defense. Besides, you and I both know he needed killing." Jimmy shifted his arm in the sling.

Morris stared out the window at the snow-covered mountains looming to the west. "It's not that simple. The newspapers don't know Nodacker was on the take—and

48

they're not going to know. That leaves us to explain how come two Treasury agents are in a shoot out in the parking lot of the City and County Building. Got any ideas what to tell them? Jimmy, there's just one thing to do, and I've already done it. As of now you're transferred to our Honolulu office. I'll make up some cock and bull story to cover things here. As for you, I've got a car waiting to drive you to Grand Junction. You can catch the train to Los Angeles there. The Dollar Line boat for Honolulu leaves L.A. next Tuesday. Here's the tickets. I asked Billy and Connie to pack a bag for you. And here's an envelope with enough cash to pose as a big-time gambler on the boat. After you're in Honolulu, keep up the cover. Wait for the Treasury Office to contact you. Connie's here. She wants to say good-bye before you and Billy leave."

Morris opened the door to the hospital room. Connie stood outside. As he left, Morris turned back to Jimmy. "Don't be long. We've got to get you out of here."

"I know you have to go quickly. I just wanted to say good-bye. Please be careful, Jimmy." Connie kissed him and held on tight.

"I'll be back, Connie, and when I am we'll get Tanner once and for all."

Connie stiffened and stepped back. "You'll get Tanner? Jimmy, how can you still talk that way? How many people have to die?"

"Do you want me to forget Jolly? Should we pretend Tanner's hoods didn't blow him in two with a shotgun?"

Connie's eyes blazed. "Jolly wouldn't be dead if he hadn't been chasing down a tip for you!"

"Connie, say what you want, but I'm getting Tanner, with or without you or anybody else."

Connie spoke slowly and carefully. "Then good-bye,

Jimmy; good-bye until you come to your senses. I've had enough." She walked through the door and down the hospital corridor.

Morris came back up the corridor, followed by Billy Bonnie. "It's time to go. Move it! The newspaper boys are all over the place downstairs."

Jimmy confronted Billy. "Why are you going? I'm the one in trouble."

Billy grinned, "Well, I figured somebody'd have to look after you. You're sure no good at looking after yourself."

"C'mon, c'mon. Let's go." Morris hurried toward the back stairs and the waiting car on the street below.

* * *

The Denver Zephyr put them in Los Angeles on Monday afternoon. The boat was scheduled to leave from the Dollar Line pier late Tuesday morning. Billy and Jimmy wound up in Long Beach with the night ahead of them. Jimmy's shoulder had improved enough for him to discard the sling.

As the evening wore on, they drank themselves from place to place. By midnight they reached a place called the Blue Grotto and settled in for some serious drinking.

"To Honolulu, land of orchids and bare-breasted women," Billy raised his glass.

"*Honolulu, for Chrissake*," Jimmy thought. After coming so close to nailing Tanner, it was like being exiled on the moon. He felt reckless enough to jump the first train back to Denver.

"Honolulu? Why I've always dreamed of going there!" a voice interrupted.

Jimmy and Billy looked up at the waitress who'd just

brought them another round. Her nameplate read "Dee" and she was a long, leggy blonde. She wouldn't have any trouble measuring up to the beauty of the native girls in any island paradise. By two o'clock that morning, Billy was off on his own and Jimmy had accepted an invitation to Dee's bungalow in Venice.

"What do you do?"

"I'm a businessman."

"You don't look like a businessman. What kind of business are you in?"

"Mostly monkey business."

"Come on, Jimmy, what do you do?"

"Make love to beautiful girls."

The night passed quickly and Jimmy, feeling considerably less reckless and more rocky than anything else, was cleaning up the next morning to make a dash for the boat to Honolulu. He would meet Billy on the pier. Splashing icy water on his face, he opened the medicine cabinet to look for a razor, if there was one. Instead, he found a short section of rubber tubing and a syringe.

Dee was leaning against the door jamb watching him.

"Morphine?" he asked abruptly. She nodded casually.

"That stuff will kill you, honey. Better lay off."

Dee gathered her dressing gown around her and lit a cigarette. "I can stop when I want. But it sure makes the world a beautiful place. You ought to try it sometime."

"How did you get started?"

"I had a boyfriend who was a doctor."

"What happened to him?"

"He's dead now."

"Make sure that doesn't happen to you. You're too nice to wind up on a slab."

51

"You're nice too, Jimmy. You're nicer to me than any-body I've met for a long time. Sure you can't stay over for a day or two?"

"I've got a partner expecting me to meet him at the boat. Got to go."

"Can I write you at the Royal Hawaiian?"

"Sure. So long, kid. Watch that dope—it'll get you."

"You didn't seem to mind how I was acting last night, Jimmy."

"You're great, honey. Just watch yourself."

Jimmy kissed Dee good-bye as the cab drove up outside the bungalow.

\* \* \*

Billy stood on the balcony of their suite at the Royal Hawaiian, looking out on the rolling Pacific. The late afternoon light gave a rosy tint to the curve of the beach at Waikiki. "I could get to like this life, Jimmy. It sure beats working. We've been here a week, spending money like it was going out of style. Nothing to do but have a big time every night. When do you suppose the Treasury office is going to contact us?"

Jimmy joined his partner on the balcony. "Probably not until our cover is really in place. Still, you'd think they would at least give us some kind of a sign of what we're supposed to be doing."

There was a message at the desk when they came down for the evening, but not from Honolulu Treasury. It was a cryptic telegram from Tom Morris:

**L SAYS BE LOOKING FOR CHINAMAN STOP**
(signed) Morris

"What the hell is this? What Chinaman? Who is 'L'? Where are we supposed to be looking?"

As they turned from the hotel desk, Billy and Jimmy were approached by a tall, thin man who said, "Treasury wants to see you guys. There's a car outside."

The trip downtown gave Billy and Jimmy no information from the thin man or from his partner who was driving the car. Once downtown they were ushered into the back room of a small Chinese restaurant four blocks from the beach. A bald, fat man sat at a small table under the light, smoking a cigarette. Matt Hogan, the Treasury chief for Honolulu, began talking without waiting for introductions, waving a copy of the telegram Billy and Jimmy had received at the Royal Hawaiian. "I need some answers. Who is 'L'? Who's the Chinaman? What have you guys been doing?"

Jimmy answered as they sat down. "We're here because we were sent from Denver. We don't know who 'L' or the Chinaman might be. To tell you the truth we figured you were going to tell us the answers to some of those questions."

"Don't give me that. You got sent here because you were in trouble in Denver. I don't want you here messing up our work. I'll be happy when you go back where you came from. Meanwhile, I don't like wise guys who go off on their own. Now who is 'L'? Who's the Chinaman?"

Jimmy bristled, "How the hell should we know? Besides, who asked you to snoop into our messages?"

Hogan flushed, ground out his cigarette and stood up. "Okay, wise guy. So you say you don't know what's in that telegram. Well, here's a piece of information you can put in the bank. I didn't want you two here in the first place.

I'm going to ship your ass back to Denver as soon as I can. Meanwhile, watch your step and stay out of my hair. If I get the idea that you're playing games with me, that you do know about 'L' or the Chinaman or anything else, I'll put you in jail, so help me. Now get out of my hair—and stay out."

As they walked through the streets of downtown Honolulu, teeming with lights and people in the warm, humid twilight of an early evening, Billy and Jimmy pondered their strange interview.

"What the hell was all that about, Jimmy? First that screwy telegram, then the hostile reaction from the Treasury guy! Now what?"

"Billy, I think the Treasury office just doesn't want anything going on they can't control. They think we're pulling some fast one on 'em. We'd probably feel the same way if the tables were turned."

"Okay, Jimmy—okay—but what does the telegram mean?"

Jimmy and Billy wandered into a restaurant and ordered dinner. The courtyard where they ate was open to the street outside and the sounds of the evening drifted in as they talked.

Jimmy pushed back his plate. "I don't know about this 'Chinaman' business, but I think that 'L' must be a tipster. Who do we know who has an inside connection, who's helped us before, and who has a last name starting with 'L'?"

Billy's face lit up instantly. "Tom Leahy! It's got to be."

Jimmy said, "I hate to admit it, but it looks like Leahy *is* on our side. That's got to be who Morris meant in the telegram. Now what's this stuff about 'the Chinaman'? Somehow this is a tip that Leahy has picked up inside the Denver Police Department, something to do with Tanner, something we can do something about in Honolulu."

The next two days brought no answers. Twice Billy and Jimmy were aware that they were being tailed. But since they were just killing time, with no real idea of where to look or what to do, it didn't seem to matter much whether they were being tailed by Treasury or not.

On the morning of the third day, another telegram was waiting at the Royal Hawaiian desk:

L DEAD STOP LAST MESSAGE BEFORE
SHOOTING SAID CHINAMAN AT
HALEKALANI STOP WILL HAVE PACKAGE
STOP CHECK AND ADVISE STOP
    (signed) Morris

As Jimmy read the note, he headed for the door. "Get a cab, Billy. We've got to move before Honolulu Treasury gets a copy of this telegram."

Entering the cab outside the hotel, Billy saw the thin man and his partner rush from the lobby and head for their car. "Here's an extra twenty bucks to lose that car before you take us to the Halekalani. Step on it!"

Their cabby led the Treasury tail on a wild goose chase behind Diamond Head, then doubled back toward downtown, delivering Billy and Jimmy at the old Halekalani Hotel in the very heart of Waikiki. There was no sign of Treasury agents from the Honolulu office. As they entered the Halekalani lobby, Jimmy said, "We'd better find this Chinaman fast. Treasury will be picking up a copy of that telegram soon and they'll be down here right on top of us about ten minutes later."

Billy hesitated as he looked around the lobby. "How the

hell do I know *which* Chinaman we're looking for? Honolulu's filled with 'em. I'll bet I can see half a dozen in this lobby right now!"

"Please come with me quickly. We have only a few moments. I must not be here when Hogan and his men arrive." The elderly Oriental had risen from a couch near the entrance to the Halekalani lobby. "You are Bonnie and Carr, are you not?" A moment later the three men had entered a small back room in the hotel. "This box contains the information you seek." The Chinaman placed a small, lacquer box on the table.

Jimmy started to open the box. "What is this? Who are you?"

"I am a former business associate of Mr. Tanner. We and our partners had joint operations in Honolulu, San Francisco, and Denver. Mr. Tanner has not taken good care of his partners, and now we repay his treachery by providing the information which you seek. I must go now. I am the last surviving partner besides Mr. Tanner. Only he will be hurt by the contents of this box. But I must not fall into the hands of Honolulu Treasury. My life would be worthless." The Chinaman was gone as quickly as he had come.

As they started to leave the room, Billy spotted Hogan and the other Treasury agents at the main hotel entrance across the Halekalani lobby. "Quick, out the back way! We got to get rid of this box before they grab us."

Ducking out a hotel service entrance, Billy and Jimmy lost themselves in the crowded Honolulu streets. Stopping for a moment in a pawn shop, they hocked the small, lacquer box. Then they mailed the pawn ticket and the key to the box to themselves, care of General Delivery, Honolulu. "At least they won't find the pawn ticket on us," Billy breathed as they dropped the letter in a downtown mailbox.

Billy and Jimmy deliberately spent the day drifting around downtown Honolulu, because they expected Treasury to be waiting at the Royal Hawaiian. When they returned to the hotel around seven p.m., Hogan and his men were waiting in their suite.

"Well, if it isn't my smart-ass buddies! Where have you been boys, Chinatown?" Hogan sat on the couch, facing a coffee table full of cigarette butts. "We were getting tired of waiting for you. Thanks for dropping in."

Jimmy looked around the room. "We thought we'd play tourist and check out your island paradise."

"Shut up, wise guy, before I shut you up," Hogan growled. "Now let's have it. Who was 'L', where is the Chinaman and where is that package? I want to know and I want to know now." Hogan waved a copy of the second telegram.

Billy and Jimmy exchanged glances. They had spent the afternoon thinking through what they could expect and had decided that should the box fall in Hogan's hands, their last chance to get Tanner would be gone.

Jimmy spoke first. "The Chinaman didn't show, so there wasn't any package. As for the identity of 'L', your guess is as good as ours. Apparently he was some stoolie that got caught."

"Okay, wise guy, have it your way. Let me ask you another question. Who is Dee? You got another telegram while you were out this afternoon. This one was sent from a ship. Hogan tossed a telegram on the coffee table:

ACCEPTING YOUR INVITATION TO VISIT
ROYAL HAWAIIAN STOP ARRIVING

WEDNESDAY STOP CANNOT WAIT
TO SEE YOU STOP LOVE STOP
(signed) Dee

"Now let's have it, wise guy. Who's Dee?"

Jimmy sputtered, "Look, I didn't have anything to do with this. Dee's some gal I met in Long Beach before we came to Honolulu. If she's coming, she's coming on her own."

"Yeah, well let me tell you something wise guy. Did you ever hear of the Mann Act? It's a crime to transport women across state lines for immoral purposes. If I don't have the Chinaman's identity and that package before that boat arrives in four days, you're going to jail on the Mann Act."

"You can't do that!"

"The hell I can't. You just watch me!" Hogan and his Treasury men headed for the door. "Don't bother to get up; we can let ourselves out. Incidentally, don't try to skip. We'll be watching you every minute."

Billy stared at the closed hotel door. "Now what, Jimmy? Is this Dee the gal you spent the night with, the one we met at the Blue Grotto in Long Beach?"

Jimmy sat without moving a muscle. "Yeah, she's the one. My God, Billy, I didn't tell the crazy broad to come to Honolulu. What am I going to do?"

The next several days left Billy and Jimmy always in their suite, trying to decide what to do. By the morning of the fourth day they had it figured. They couldn't give Hogan the box without risking their case against Tanner. They couldn't tell Hogan about the Chinaman because they didn't know who he was or where he was. They believed Hogan meant his threat to charge Jimmy under the Mann Act.

58

"There's only one thing to do, Billy. Meet the boat and marry Dee. Then I'm sure as hell not transporting her for immoral purposes! When we get to L.A., I'll annul the marriage and we'll get back to Denver with the goods on Tanner."

"I know, Jimmy—but, my God, marry her?"

"It's all we can do. The boat docks in two hours. Arrange for a preacher to meet us at the dock. We hold the ceremony right under Hogan's nose. Send a messenger to get that pawn ticket and key in General Delivery. Then send another messenger to pick up the box. Then have him take the box to a flower shop. Arrange with the florist for the biggest batch of flowers they've ever seen and have 'em build the box and key right into the middle of the flower arrangement. Have the flowers delivered right to the dockside ceremony. Book return passage with Dollar Line for the three of us, on the condition that we can board the boat immediately after the wedding ceremony and stay on board 'til the boat sails. And get ready to give Hogan the finger as the boat pulls away from the dock!"

"God, Jimmy, do you think it'll work?"

"Billy, it's got to."

Jimmy was right. It had to work—and it did. Dee came down the gangplank in a haze of morphine and accepted the proposal of marriage as though she'd been expecting it all along. Hogan and his men stood by with their mouths open as the ceremony took place. Billy was the best man. Within ten minutes the happy wedding party was on its way up the gangplank amid an ocean of flowers. Hogan's men took Billy's and Jimmy's luggage completely apart and finally gave up the search in disgust.

"You ever come back to Honolulu, you son of a bitch, and I'll lock you up for sure."

Jimmy, Billy, and Dee waved from the deck as the radiant bride peeked over the mountain of flowers she held. "Aloha, Hogan!" Jimmy shouted.

*   *   *

The boat trip was one continual high in the aftermath of the victory over Hogan. The first night on board had led to an investigation of the lacquer box and its contents—filled with enough names, places, dates, and account numbers to put Tanner and his henchmen away forever.

Billy and Jimmy were feeling great and Dee made good company from the beginning. "I understand, Jimmy. Gosh, I never expected us to get married, so there's no reason I should expect us to stay married. I'm just glad to be needed. It's been so long since anybody gave a damn about me that it's nice to be needed, nice to have a friend."

The five days flew by—tomorrow they would dock in Los Angeles. "Jimmy, let me come to Denver with you. I won't be any trouble. I won't try to sleep with you. I won't try to change your mind. Please, Jimmy. Let me stay with you for a few more days."

Jimmy agreed. The last night on shipboard, Billy warned him that no matter what her promises were, Dee was falling in love with him. "You'd better watch it, Jimmy. Dee is going to stick to you like a mustard plaster."

"She'll be all right. Give her a break. A few more days won't hurt anybody." Jimmy reassured Billy, but he wondered—what would happen when the time came to say good-bye?

The Zephyr left L.A. in late afternoon, heading east toward Denver. They were scheduled to arrive at eleven-thirty the next night. Billy had wired Tom Morris to meet the train with his agents and take charge of the lacquer box. The time hurried by as Dee began to talk about her life. Something about the look in her eyes told Billy he was right. Dee was falling in love with Jimmy. It might be a huge joke to everybody else, but Dee had found someone who was nice to her, someone whom she loved, who might—just might—love her. Mile after mile, the feeling grew.

When the California Zephyr arrived in Denver's Union Station on that dark May night, Billy and Jimmy watched the platform closely for signs of Tom Morris and his Treasury agents. They were not in sight. The platform seemed completely deserted. The pools of yellow light from the overhead lamps were all empty.

"Where the hell is Morris? He was supposed to meet this train." Jimmy checked again as the train drew to a stop.

"He said he'd be here, so he'll be here," Billy replied. "Let's get off the train. Come on, Dee. Welcome to Denver."

As Billy stepped from the train and turned to offer Dee a hand, he did not see Rugg Tanner and the three men with him as they stepped from the shadows. Tanner fired first, striking Billy between the shoulder blades. Jimmy was still on the train, holding the lacquer box and standing behind Dee as she stepped to the platform. At the first shot, Jimmy reached for his shoulder holster.

In the hail of bullets which followed, Jimmy fired at Tanner, striking him in the groin. As Jimmy tried to pull Dee back inside the train, she was struck three times by bullets intended for Jimmy. Two more shots knocked Jimmy over backward. Bleeding from wounds in his side and leg, Jimmy emptied his automatic into the group of men behind Tanner. Tom Morris and his agents appeared from the shadows and began firing from both ends of the platform. Tanner and all three men with him were down. The gunfight was over.

\* \* \*

Jimmy was back in another hospital bed. Tom Morris sat in a chair at his bedside.

"Why did Tanner try to pull such a stunt?" Jimmy asked.

"He had to. If we ever got that lacquer box to court, he was through and he knew it. If he let you and Billy live, he was through anyway, because you had both seen the evidence and could testify. He had to kill you. Besides," Morris continued, "Rugg Tanner had been a law unto himself for so long, he got to thinking nobody could stop him. I don't know how the hell he knew you were coming. We should have given you guys better protection."

"It's not your fault, Tom. Too many things were happening at once. I guess we'll never know everything that happened or why it happened. You know, Tom, we'd never have nailed Tanner without Leahy's information. What happened to him?"

Morris sighed, "Like I wired you, he was shot and killed. Tanner must have tumbled to what Leahy was doing and killed him. Now Tanner's dead, too. I guess it was the lacquer box that really killed him."

Jimmy looked out the hospital window. "Leahy was a good man. I'm sorry I didn't get to tell him so."

"Lots of good men are dead, Jimmy. Billy never knew what hit him. And that girl who helped you smuggle the lacquer box out of Honolulu. Jimmy, I think she took some of the bullets that might have killed you if she hadn't been in the way."

"It turns out I really needed Dee after all. That's what she wanted—to be needed," Jimmy murmured.

"What?"

"Nothing. Just thinking about something she said to me."

"Well, good-bye Jimmy. I've got to go. Besides, you've got another visitor. Father Horrigan is outside."

"I'd like to see him. Oh, hello Father—please come in. Good-bye, Tom. Thanks for everything."

The tall, angular old priest sat down in the chair next to the bed. "Well, Jimmy, are you tired of getting shot?"

"I sure am. I'm tired of a lot of things."

"What about law school? Will you be going back now? I saw Connie the other day and she was asking."

"Maybe so, Father. But I've got some things to straighten out in my mind first."

"Like what, Jimmy?"

"Like Jolly Prance, Tom Leahy, Billy, Dee."

Father Horrigan looked straight at Jimmy. "Is Dee the young woman who helped you with Tanner, the one who was shot on the train platform?"

"She's the one, Father. And now they're all dead, dead because I was determined to get Tanner. They're all dead, Father. Billy would be alive if it weren't for me."

"You did what you thought was right, Jimmy. So did Billy—now let it rest. God expects you to do what you must do. He wants His creatures to make good choices and stick with those choices. But when you're finished with a job, finished with a piece of your life, let it go.

What's done is done. Now you've got to decide what comes next. That's what being a human being is all about. And one other thing, Jimmy—"

"Yes, Father?"

"God's always there to help you with the next choice."

# Adobe Park

ROSS Cieth was a big man. He had a bushy, black moustache, a pock-marked face, and a pair of deep-set eyes that looked right through you. He was never loud or pushy, but he gave out a feeling of power under restraint, a sense that he was a good man to leave alone. I was a small boy when I first saw him. Ross had been hired by my dad to help out around the store in Colorado Springs, making deliveries, repairing appliances, and acting as general handyman.

After Dad's heart attack, we needed help at the store. Business was getting a little better by 1939 and with his ability to work so greatly reduced, Mom, my big sister, and I were having a harder and harder time trying to keep up. When my grandad retired from the Post Office in Denver the year before, he and my grandmother moved to Colorado Springs to help out, but we really needed the kind of help that Ross brought when he showed up in answer to an ad Dad ran in the newspaper.

Ross was so quiet that at first none of us really got to know him. He kept to his work and never seemed to have much to say, especially about himself. He was a hard worker, always polite and accommodating. Things went a lot better at the store during the next year. We all came to depend on Ross and were sure glad he'd answered that ad. Right off the bat, Ross was truthful. He told Dad he was an ex-con who had killed a man in a fight. But from the forthright way he said it, you would find it hard to believe that he was untrustworthy. Some men just are and you know it instinctively. Nowadays to get hired you have to show your social security card and give references; Dad just smiled and said, "When can you start?" For him, Ross' past was dead and buried and he was glad to leave it that way.

It was one day in late May 1941 that my dad got us all together in the kitchen and said he had something to tell us. He was really excited and looked better than at any time since he'd been in the hospital. "We're buying a ranch—up above Salida in a place called Adobe Park—160 acres, horses, cows, the works!"

All the usual questions came up: What did we know about ranching? What were we going to use for money to buy the place? But it was obvious from the first that we all wanted to go. Dad had arranged a loan. In those days there were so many farms going begging with uncollected mortgages that about all you had to do was sign your name and promise to make the payments. Besides, we had accumulated a pretty good stake in the store. As for knowing how to run a ranch, Dad said we'd learn what we needed to know as a family.

"What about Dad's health?" my sister asked.

"I can do it. Working outside will be good for me."

By the time Dad was through talking, we were ready to go, even Gramaw and Grandad.

Mom had said nothing throughout the discussion. That was her way. If she had something to say, especially something to argue about, she'd wait until she and Dad were alone. Sometimes I could just barely hear them when I was very quiet in bed.

"Peter, why leave Colorado Springs? We're making a little money at the store. We're all together. Your folks are with us now. Why run the risk of a hard life on a ranch, especially after the doctor warned you that you couldn't work anymore?"

"But I *can* work, Fran! I've been getting stronger for the last year. I've been doing more and more in the store. I can do it!"

"You don't *need* to do it," Mom interrupted. "Why tempt fate? Why can't you ever be satisfied?"

"Because of the kids. They deserve a chance for something besides this damn store!" Dad responded.

"You're such a dreamer—you're always looking for some magic land where everything will be perfect. Why don't you grow up?"

"I don't know what you call 'growing up.' But I do know our son and daughter are missing out on a lot of the experiences that mean *real* growing up," Dad bristled. "The way the world is going, those kids will need roots more desperately than any generation before—far worse than you and I did. There's only one place to find those roots: the land. We've got to give them a chance, a real chance, to earn their living and their self-respect, to build something lasting to pass on to *their* children. That's all we can give them—roots."

"Good Lord, Peter, be a visionary if you must, but don't punish your family!"

Dad answered very slowly and quietly, "Fran, when I was in the hospital and didn't expect to live, the main thought I had was that I'd let the kids down—that I wasn't leaving them with what they were going to need. I'm convinced that the best thing I can give the family, you included, is a sense of purpose, a sense of belonging. This ranch is the only chance I know to do that. Please help me."

"Peter, you know I will. I don't know whether you're right or not. Sometimes you scare me. But you know I love you. If this is what you want, we'll do it together."

That was the last sound I heard that night. As a little boy, I hadn't fully understood what was being discussed, but I did understand that whatever we were doing, we were doing it together as a family. Adobe Park, here we come!

Dad invited Ross to move with us when we left in early June. He didn't say much, but he seemed glad that the family had asked him to come along. He had been with us long enough that he seemed more like family than hired help. Besides, we all knew that we were likely to need his help badly at the ranch.

We loaded the old truck Dad had borrowed until we couldn't pile it any higher, then we set out for Adobe Park. Dad and Ross drove the truck. Mom, Gramaw, Grandad, my sister Frannie and I followed in the family car. It was only about a hundred miles to the upper Arkansas Valley, but the old truck was mighty slow. Frannie and I hadn't seen the ranch and we were about to pop with suspense waiting for our first look.

It was late afternoon when we finally arrived. I'd never seen the upper Arkansas Valley before. The Mosquito Range formed one side of the long narrow valley through which the Arkansas River flowed. The other side of the valley was framed by the Saquache Mountains, some of the tallest 14,000 foot peaks in the state. On the Saquache side of the valley, nestled high in the pinon pines sloping down toward the river, was the place called Adobe Park. Our ranch was smack dab in the middle, right at the foot of Mt. Shavano.

We followed the truck up the dirt road leading from the paved highway. Frannie and I were out of the car almost before it stopped. The mountain towered over the little ranch house with the pump outside. The ice house was dug into a hill a few yards away.

The barn and corral were just over another hill right behind the house. The whole place was on a high ground surrounded by pinon pines, overlooking a valley which sloped away across the paved highway, running down the hill to the river. The late summer twilight gave Frannie and me a good, long chance to check things out. For two city kids, the ranch looked like a pretty exciting place.

From the start, we were short on money and long on plans. Everything needed to be fixed or replaced. The house needed work; wood, a lot of wood, had to be cut in preparation for winter; the alfalfa planting was already late; the irrigation ditches running through deep cuts in the pinon hills were half-blocked with cave-ins; the ice-house was a mess; the stock was mostly nonexistent; the old steel-lugged tractor was completely frozen up from years of neglect. But the place looked good to us.

Everybody pitched in that summer. Dad was a good mechanic and he had that old steel-lugged tractor going before long. The alfalfa came next. He plowed and planted from first sun to last light and then rigged kerosene lanterns on the front of the tractor to keep going long after dark.

Ross and Grandad worked long and hard, cleaning the ditches that ran through those pinon cuts. It was dangerous work, because new cave-ins from the clay banks hanging thirty feet overhead could (and sometimes did) come crashing down anytime. It was hard work, too, hard even for a big man like Ross. He would come home at dark dragging his tail, covered with adobe and completely done in. I don't know how an old man like Grandad kept up the pace. I think he was just too stubborn to quit. Some days almost killed him, but he was determined that he was going to stay with the job.

Mom and Gramaw worked with that wreck of a house, got the wood stove working, did their own carpentry work on the windows to close up the holes before winter, planted and tended a big garden and managed to fix the meals, tend the chickens, feed the hogs and generally keep us all going.

Frannie and I at nine and five were big enough to help with the garden, feed the animals, and gather wood. My Lord, did we gather wood! Fallen pinon was everywhere and our job was to drag it in and make a big pile—a *big* pile—to get ready for the cutting and stacking which had to be finished before fall. No matter how big the pile got, Grandad was always on us to make it bigger. "You call that a woodpile? You haven't even got a good start! What do you two do all day? I want to see some results tomorrow." I got so I dreamed about that damn woodpile.

One way or another, we made it through that first summer. Things started taking shape. Everybody worked hard, but nobody harder than Dad. There were some times he just couldn't seem to get enough air into his lungs to keep going. He'd have to stop and gasp for air until he got his breath. Then he'd start in again. Each day he seemed a little stronger—and the work got done.

Even old Grandad appeared to have mellowed. He

seemed to feel good knowing that he was doing a man's work. As for Ross, he had never been around anything like the ranch in his whole life, but he was learning. I think he was glad to have a family and a chance to work and help. Mom did best of all. She didn't have two dimes to rub together, worked all day and half the night, and still always had time for a smile for any of us, especially for Frannie and me.

That fall we continued to gather and cut wood. That pile of pinon was the biggest I've ever seen. We used the power takeoff on the old tractor to turn the saw and we cut and stacked, cut and stacked. The whole family did that job together. When we were through, we still didn't have much money, but we sure weren't going to be cold for the winter.

The main stock were a few white-face cattle, but we kept one milk cow. We also slopped two pigs, Madam Queen and Sadie, looking forward to some pork chops somewhere down the road. When we finally did butcher, we had some great meat. Grandad was really funny about that meat, though. When he saw that hog dressed out, he wouldn't eat any. He was a city boy and his pork chops had to come from the store.

There were three horses on the place when we came, Polly, Molly, and the workhorse, Big Dick. Polly and Molly were two small roans not good for much except a saddle or pulling a small cart. Big Dick was a huge work-horse who filled in more than once when the tractor broke down. The big black killed himself that first winter when he got into the grain and foundered. We had to drag him out of the barn with the tractor. By the time we had Big Dick out in the pinon woods, he was swollen to twice his normal size. We needed the five dollars for the hide, but every time my dad would try to skin him, the escaping gas would drive him away. Finally Frannie and I crouched down with Dad about fifty feet away while he plincked the carcass with a .22 rifle. He was trying to let that gas escape so that he could skin him. Didn't work: Every time there would be a little spurt of gas from the new hole, then the hole would plug with the bloat from inside the hide— about like a puncture-proof tire. Dad finally had to skin him, bloat and all. He wrapped his nose and mouth in a big towel. "Toughest five dollars I ever earned," he gasped as he finally stumbled away with that hide.

My animal troubles were different. There was a burro on the ranch when we came. His name was Smoky. He was so much smarter than I that it wasn't even funny. Smoky could let himself in and out of the corral any time he wanted. He'd tolerate Frannie or me on his back (usually), and that's what finally got me in trouble. It was my turn to go riding with Ross, who went out with Frannie and me occasionally.

Anyway, I was following Ross and the little roan Molly, or maybe I should say Smoky was following Ross and Molly. I just happened to be on Smoky's back at the time. When Ross headed down a steep hill on the way home, I tried to talk him out of it, but he just kept going. Smoky followed, paying no attention to me. As we passed under a low-hanging pinon branch, I grabbed hold in fright. Smoky kept right on going and walked out from under me. As soon as my weight was on the dead branch, down I went, right into a bed of cactus. I dropped right behind Smoky's hooves. It's a good thing he was a burro, not a horse, or I would probably have had my head kicked off.

Ross scooped me up and took me home. I was full of cactus. That night I was the main attraction. I was sitting naked in a washtub of baking soda water, while Mom, Dad, Gramaw, and Grandad (each with tweezers) picked cactus from me by the light of two kerosene lamps. Who says there was no home entertainment before television?

That winter we cut ice for the icehouse. The little pond we worked on wasn't far from the house. We'd had an early freeze and not much snow, so it wasn't really hard to cut ice so long as we remembered to saw the chunks small enough to be able to carry them to the sledge. Without Big Dick, we had to use Molly and Polly to haul the sledge. Polly was a little crazy as usual, but she settled down and we filled the icehouse dug into the side of the hill. The problem we never licked, that year or ever, was finding a way to keep the water dogs out of the ice. At least we called them water dogs. They looked like a cross between a fish and a rat and sure didn't do anything to make the ice more attractive. The sight of one of those things frozen dead in the ice sort of made you lose interest in lemonade. Still, the ice was a big help for lots of things since we didn't have any electricity.

Christmas was great that year. We cut our own tree about half a mile from the house and dragged it back through the snow. Mom made some decorations. We didn't have much in the way of presents, but we had a warm house and plenty to eat. On New Year's Eve, the full moon was shining on the snow, outlining Mt. Shavano towering above us. The cold was sharp and held the smoke from the chimney low as it drifted down the valley. I wanted to stay up till midnight, but I fell asleep. As the new year drew close, Dad shook me awake. When I cleared my eyes, everybody held hands and sang "Auld Lang Syne." Dad's eyes filled with tears and he turned away. Every New Year we sang that song and every New

Year Dad would come as close to crying as he ever came. Once I asked him why. He said the song and the end of another year with his family always made him think how lucky he was. "Tears of joy, son, tears of joy."

The next summer we went to Denver for a few things. We were settled on the ranch. The chickens, the cows, and the alfalfa were our cash crop. We weren't spending much, what with being able to feed and house ourselves for just about nothing. So we were able to pay on the mortgage and even had a little for the trip to Denver. On the way through Morrison, we had a chance to pick up a suckling pig which we took home to fatten up for a special dinner. It seemed like a good idea at the time, but the smell on the trip home was awful.

That was the summer we had the ice cream social. We had a lot of extra cream in the ice house and a load of cherries that were about ripe, so we decided to invite the neighboring ranchers for some ice cream. We didn't know until early that Sunday morning that the cream had gone blinky. It was too late to call everybody (even if we had a phone), so my dad just kept tinkering with the mix, adding sugar, adding cherries. We kept getting a bigger batch, but it didn't cover the blinky cream. Everybody in the valley was nice about it, eating a few bites, looking at one another, and then eating a few more bites. Once you got used to the taste, it really wasn't so bad.

That summer we didn't have very good luck with the chickens, either. We sold a lot of frying chickens to Jenny's Fried Chicken Diner in Salida. She'd been a good customer, so we tried to oblige when she needed a big batch of chickens at a time when we weren't ready with a new crop. We fed those little buggers and fed them and fed them, but when we dressed them out, they were all craw and no body. Jenny was so mad when she saw them that we lost a good customer for a while.

We also had a little trouble with the state police that summer. About eighty acres of our alfalfa land was on the other side of the paved highway and to work it Dad had to cross the road with the old, steel-lugged tractor. This always left a row of triangular holes running across the pavement and was guaranteed to get the state troopers excited. When we saw that white cruiser coming up the drive, we always knew right away what he wanted. He told Dad not to do that anymore—I think the trooper knew good and well that Dad would still go over there and work his land. We tried laying boards across the road to keep the old tractor from sinking into the pavement, but somehow the holes were still there.

That fall was my first year in school. Frannie was four years ahead of me and had been in Adobe Park School the year before as a fourth grader. She didn't like it much and when I got there the next year I could see why. The young teacher was fresh from college and she just wasn't tough enough to handle those big ranch boys who were going to be in that school forever unless the school district finally gave up trying to educate them. The teacher could handle the fifth graders like Frannie and the first graders like me, but those four Leach brothers were all bunched together some place between the sixth and eighth grades and weren't taking their grades for the first time either. Each brother from the Leach ranch outweighed the teacher by a good fifty pounds. Looking back on it, I don't see how she had the guts to show up in the morning. The Leaches terrorized the little kids, did as they pleased, flooded the school yard so that it froze one weekend and then laughed till they cried when the teacher had to crawl over the ice on her hands and knees to get into the school Monday morning.

I don't know what I learned that year in school, except that I had a good sister. One day the Leach boys were terrorizing everybody as usual in the school yard when one of them gave me a bat behind the ear and knocked me down. Frannie walked up to him and slugged him right in the eye. About two seconds later, all the Leach brothers were knocking her around. They had her down and were stuffing dirt in her mouth and rubbing it in her eyes. I jumped on the pile and bit one of them on the calf. I can't say it helped Frannie much, but it earned me a few bruises and my own mouthful of dirt.

That night we were a sorry mess walking the mile up the dirt road to our place. Mom took one look and called Dad, Grandad and Ross into the house. Dad asked a question or two, then the three of them piled in the car and drove away. I guess they went to Leaches. I never heard any of them talk about it, but the Leach boys never touched us again.

Maybe that trouble with the Leaches started the rest of the trouble. I don't know. But I was along the day we made the trip to Salida when the real trouble started. My grandparents were back in Denver by then, but Dad, Mom, Ross, Frannie and I were all along that Saturday when we went to town. It was kind of a treat for all of us to go to town, especially for Mom. We had run a few errands at the drugstore and the hardware store and had delivered some dressed chickens at Jenny's. On the way out of town we stopped for a drink at the Crossroads, a bar at the junction of US 285 and US 50 where 50 heads west to go over Monarch Pass.

The father and two uncles of the Leach boys were

sitting with several hangers-on in one corner of the bar. You could feel the air thicken when we walked in.

One of the Leaches spoke up. "Well, if it ain't the jail bird! Did they let you out for the day? What's the matter, ain't you found any sick people lying around for you to beat to death?"

In a very quiet voice, Dad told Mom to take Frannie and me and wait in the car, but as we got up to leave, one of the Leaches started around the end of the bar. Dad met him as he came and slammed him into a table. In about a second, the rest of the Leaches and two of their friends were there. Dad and Ross met them head-on. Mom pulled Frannie and me back to the wall.

For a couple of minutes the action was fast and furious. Everybody got knocked around some and the Crossroads lost quite a bit in the furniture department. One thing that impressed me as a little kid that day is that fights like that don't last long—they're just too rough to go on. The bartender pulled a .38 from under the counter and shot twice into the ceiling. That got everybody's attention. The fight was over.

The bartender waved that Police Special. "When I tote up the damage, I'll expect each side to pay half. Now get the hell out of here before the sheriff comes. I don't need any more trouble."

That pretty well ended it with the Leaches. I guess nobody wanted any more trouble. We couldn't figure how Ross' record had surfaced in Salida, but it was out.

From the little bit I ever heard my folks say, Ross had a good reason for the fight in which he had accidentally killed a man. Ross himself never talked about it around us kids. I do know that we all considered him family. For us, the past was dead and buried and we were glad Ross was with us. From then on, though, it was never the same for Ross. He couldn't get it out of his mind that he'd caused trouble for his new family.

"There's no way to fix up the past, Peter; what's done is done." I could hear Ross from the next room as I lay there in the dark pretending to sleep while the grown-ups talked late into the night. "I used to think that sooner or later I'd have paid my bill—that all the bad times would be behind me, but it's not true; it's never true. The last three years with you and your family have been great. For the first time in my life I had a family, somebody to work with and care for. I love those kids.

"Now the whole damn nightmare has come back again. I should have expected it. And I'll be damned if I'll let that hurt you and your family."

Within three weeks, that big, quiet man was on his way. None of us could talk him out of it. He was going, and that was that. He said California, but we never heard, so I don't know where he went. The last evening before he left, Frannie and I stood with Ross out by the corral and watched the sun going down behind Shavano. "Remember, kids, never let your family down—they are all you have."

Ross' departure brought us closer together as a family. We missed him, but somehow the big, quiet man was still with us.

By the next spring, we made enough payments and enough improvements on the ranch that we could refinance the mortgage. We had a real stake now. We had more than some land, some cattle and buildings, some money. We had a home for our family. Dad had been right. We had a sense of doing something that counted, a sense of belonging. That ranch is a part of our life together that I'll never forget.

I'm a grown man with kids of my own and I haven't seen Adobe Park in years, but I can still see my father riding that big, old lug tractor. He'd look up and see me standing near the edge of the fresh plowed ground in the field where he worked, wave his hand, and give me a big smile, his face filled with pride and pleasure at seeing his son.

There's no price tag on that.

# The Courtship of
# Dominic Belmonte

DOMINIC Belmonte stood in the door of the Green Parrot, watching Buena Vista come to life on Saturday morning. The long main street was bathed in October sunlight, the first customers were arriving at the hardware store, the drugstore, the grocery store. Up the street, the morning mail train was hissing steam as it prepared to head up the tracks toward Leadville. The mountains surrounding the little town were showing brilliant color. The October sun lit the yellows and reds of the aspen leaves on the high slopes. The early morning air had the strong, cold bite of fall in the high Rockies.

Dominic took a deep breath, waved at a rancher in a passing pickup truck, and stepped back inside his saloon. He had owned the Green Parrot since the mid-30s, moving from Leadville when he finally had a chance to get his own place. The last ten years had gone fast. The Green Parrot was paid off. Dom had plenty of money in the bank. He liked running the saloon, knew everybody in town—life was good. Still, Dom sometimes wondered how much longer he wanted to hang on. He'd tended bar—his own or somebody else's—for thirty years.

Maybe the time would come when enough was enough. Meanwhile, what the hell—he was doing all right.

The Green Parrot was the social hub of Buena Vista, at least for some of us. Half the weddings and most of the funerals had their last innings at that long, cool bar. Most of the town news started there. When John Henry and his wife Flossie got to arguing in the saloon and Flossie left in a huff, it was right on the street in front of the Green Parrot that John followed her out to the car and reached in the window to grab the car keys. Flossie rolled up the window on his arm above the elbow, too tight for him to get it out, then drove off up the street with John running alongside, hollering fit to be tied. Walt Fox, the town marshal, stood at the bar and pretended he didn't see what was happening. Walt was plenty tough enough when he had to step into trouble, but he'd never get between a man and his wife if he could help it.

Lots of stories like that came out of the years when Dom was running the Green Parrot. He liked most everybody and they liked him. He was generally good for a touch from the cash register when somebody needed a few bucks. When Dom had money, everybody had money. He fed anybody in town when they needed a meal. The only time he ever got mad about it was one Thanksgiving when he was cooking a turkey out in the bar kitchen. All day long he was tending bar and running back to the kitchen every few minutes to baste that turkey. The whole bar smelled with that bird and it looked like dinner was about to be served. That is, it looked like it until Dom went out to take one last look at the turkey and found out that somebody (probably one of his customers) had gone around the back way and slipped out with the bird, pan and all. They never did figure out who did it. As for Dom and the regular customers, that Thanksgiving was celebrated with a good deal less eating and a good deal more drinking than they originally planned.

Dom was generous, but he never let anybody tear up his place. Every now and then, he'd come over the bar to settle an argument with a bungstarter. Everybody still tells the story of one night when Dom came over the bar to break up a fight. One of the cowboys in that fight managed to get a hand on Dom's tie. They went round and round, but Dom couldn't shake the cowboy's hold. Before they were through, Dom had just about strangled. After that, nobody ever saw him wearing a tie again.

Years before coming to Buena Vista, he had been in another fight when he was tending bar at the Palace in Leadville. That fight cost him an eye. Once in a while, some of the regulars could get him to talk about it, and he'd give them a dose of that patented philosophizing that Dom could be counted on to supply: "I used to think I was blind in my right eye, but as I get older, I've learned that I wasn't blind at all. Really, I'd received a gift from God. He kept me from seeing all the unimportant odds and ends so that I could concentrate on *really* seeing what people are saying and doing. Now I do most of my real seeing with that 'blind' right eye. It helps me to watch what people are really up to.

"God's gifts are often misunderstood as losses, but if you're paying attention, He always gives you what you really need. All the rest is hogwash.

"I'll take what God has to give every time. What do you think any one of us has to give that can ever compare?"

That kind of philosophizing was a part of what made the Green Parrot so special for so many people in that little mountain town. Dom might be the toughest man in the house, but that short, powerful little gamecock was always thinking about something and usually had something to say that was worth hearing.

Dom was an institution, especially for Green Parrot regulars. Walt Fox, the town marshal, ranchers like Old Man Nachtrieb, and old cowboys like Lou Randall never let too many days go by between visits. Maybe that's why everybody was so amazed when Mrs. Emily Browne came to town and struck up a friendship with Dominic Belmonte. Those two seemed as far apart as two people could be. Dom was the proprietor of the best saloon in town, free and easy with his friends, ready to fight when he needed to, most everybody's idea of a great guy, but he sure wasn't the sort likely to get elected mayor in a straw vote of the ladies aid society. The Widow Browne, on the other hand, was a Denver lady who settled in Buena Vista after her husband died because his estate included a house and a little land on the edge of town. She played bridge and read books and drank tea. Nobody doubted she was a fine lady, but Dom and Widow Browne as a romantic item? Never!

Likely or not, the whole town, especially the regulars at the Green Parrot, watched a budding romance that became the main topic of conversation and the main basis of saloon bets for everybody on both sides of the tracks.

"It's like you're another guy, Dom. You're almost never here in the saloon anymore—so busy getting slicked up to go to all those tea parties you don't have any time left for your friends." Old Man Nachtrieb was having a great time giving Dominic the business. The rest of us were just sitting around waiting for something to happen. We'd all been kidding Dom, but Old Man Nachtrieb looked like

84

he might be going too far. It was beginning to look like trouble on the horizon.

"You know, Dom," Old Man Nachtrieb continued, "I've been through it all. There's not much about women that I don't know. The more you give 'em, the more they want. A woman will never be satisfied until she's made you over. Mark my words, it won't be long until she wants you to give up the Green Parrot."

Dom bristled. "Why don't you shut up, old man? Your trouble is that you drink too much—and talk too much."

Now it was Nachtrieb's turn to bristle. "Have you *ever* seen me drink enough to mess up my thinking?"

"Partner, I don't know whether or not drinking messes up your thinking. I've never seen you sober, so I don't have any basis for comparison."

For once, Old Man Nachtrieb had nothing to say. Somehow, though, I had the feeling that Dom and the widow *had* been talking about getting rid of the Green Parrot. It seemed as though he was snapping back at us because he was getting pressure to change and he wasn't sure what he wanted to do.

By Christmas that year it looked like Dom and the widow were getting married for sure. The word was out that a spring date was set for the wedding. The widow was talking around town about the plans she and "my Dominic" had made to sell the Green Parrot and retire to California after they were married. Dom didn't pay much attention to business anymore, but he'd stop by once in a while and have a nightcap after he took the widow home for the evening. One snowy, cold night, between Christmas and New Year's, he came into the bar about midnight and had a drink or two with the regulars. Old

Man Nachtrieb was there, but after the last flare-up with Dom, he wasn't saying too much about the wedding. Walt Fox never said much about anything on any subject. The old cowboy Lou Randall and I were mostly listening that night, too. Dom did most of the talking. It was the first time he'd ever said much about the whole deal.

"She wants me to sell the place and move to California," Dom muttered.

"Why would anybody want to move to California?" Old Man Nachtrieb asked sympathetically.

"Why don't you shut up, you ignorant old bastard. You don't even know where California is," Dom flared.

"I know you well enough to know that that life's not for you," Nachtrieb shot back.

"You might be right." Dom swore as he took another drink. "Hell, I don't know. I've been tending bar my whole life. Maybe it's time for a change. But I don't know if I could play bridge and make polite talk every day of my life."

"Then why not go on like you are?" Lou Randall asked.

"Because Emily says I've got to choose. It's the Green Parrot or her. I've got to decide."

Old Man Nachtrieb grunted, "That's the easiest choice I ever heard."

Dom looked him right in the eye and said, "You don't know what you're talking about. Emily's too damn nice for you to understand."

Nachtrieb took another drink. "That's for sure!"

"Well, you guys can say what you like. I've still got to decide. I can't keep putting this off. The woods are full of people who never really decide anything in their lives. You know people like that. All those vacillating bastards can do is blame one another because they can't make up their minds. A man's got to make up his mind, or he's sick. And, by God, I'm not gonna be sick until I'm dead and I'm not going to be dead until I'm buried, so you can all go to hell if you don't like it."

Walt Fox, the big, quiet marshal, never had much to say, but he spoke up now. "Hey Dom, we're not the enemy. Don't get mad at us because you've got to choose. Just make sure you can live the life that Emily's mapped out for you. If you can, go to it. If you can't, tell her so and forget the whole deal. Either way, you know damn good and well we're your friends. Besides, who says all the choices are up to you? You, me, anybody could step out that door right now and walk in front of a truck. Any time you say good-bye might be the last time. And that ought to make anybody stop and think. You got friends here, sure. We've all had some good years. But, hell, nothing's forever. You, me, everybody—we've all got to do the job all over again, every day. No matter how good yesterday was, tomorrow's only going to be as good as we make it. If you figure tomorrow's better with the widow, go to it. But stop beatin' yourself and all the rest of us so hard while you make up your mind. Now I don't know what you're doing out at this time of night, but if you'll take an old friend's advice, you'd be better off home in bed. Get out of here. Go get some sleep. We'll see you tomorrow."

Dom sat there and hesitated for just a moment. He started to say something, then he stood up, waved his hand and headed toward the door, buttoning his sheepskin as he went out into the snow. That was the last we saw of him that night, but we knew we'd hear more about Emily and the Green Parrot before it was all over.

It was about the middle of January when things finally came to a head. Dom's temper was a little shorter than

usual and one Friday night he threw out a drunken cowboy who was celebrating a little too hard. The word got
back to the widow and when she saw Dom on the street
the next day she gave him the ultimatum: no more fighting, no more Green Parrot. Dom didn't say a word. He
turned and walked off down the street.

Dom was tending bar that next night when the cowboy
he'd thrown out came back for a rematch. He was young,
he was big, and he was sober. Dom could have walked
away. He didn't. The cowboy damn near killed him.
When Walt Fox looked like he was going to step in, Dom
crawled off the floor, wiped the blood off his mouth,
waved Walt away, and waded back in. When it was all over,
Dom and the cowboy wobbled to the bar. The cocky little
man, covered with blood, bought a drink for the house.

"And fill this cowboy's glass again. This kid did me a big
favor. He reminded me that the day I quit being me, I
won't be anybody. That's reason enough to keep living.
I'm already home and I don't intend to leave."

Old Man Nachtrieb started to say something to Dom
that night at the Green Parrot, but he caught a glint of
something hard in Dom's eyes and shut his mouth. The
widow left town and went to California about ten days
later. Nobody's mentioned the widow since. The Green
Parrot's still running. Once in a while, Dom says if he has
to spend much more time with such an ignorant bunch of
cowboys, he might go to California after all.

Then he grins.

# A Helping Hand

CAL Viner came to Buena Vista about ten years ago. The first time I saw him was one day when he stopped by the newspaper office. I looked up from my desk to see a big man, tall, thick-set, maybe fifty years old—the kind of man who knows what he's doing and doesn't much care whether or not anybody else approves. It's not that Cal was arrogant. He wasn't. I never heard him raise his voice or saw him lose his temper. It was just that somehow you sensed that here was a man who knew who he was and what he was going to do.

Cal was looking for a job. Not that he wanted money— he always seemed to have all he needed. What he wanted was something to do, something that would take him out of the way of most people. You had a sense that what Cal wanted most was privacy, the more, the better. He never seemed to care how low-down the job was, so long as he could be alone while he did it. Funny thing was that Cal was obviously an educated man. He never talked about himself, but you couldn't help noticing that he had a way with words and ideas that most people just don't have.

There weren't many jobs to be had around Buena Vista in the seventies. We were a sleepy little town in the Colo-

89

rado mountains—a little mining, a few cattle, a few sheep and an annual rodeo we called Head Lettuce Days. The rodeo got its name from the lettuce fields that used to be farmed down by the Arkansas River. By the time Cal arrived, we didn't even raise lettuce anymore—I guess all that truck garden stuff had moved to California. Anyway, there wasn't much to do in or around Buena Vista when Cal Viner came to town.

Within a week, Viner had convinced one of the big sheep ranchers out in the valley that he could handle a herd on a summer drive into the high country. The Saguache mountains forming the Continental Divide to the west of Buena Vista were mostly government range where the sheepmen could run their herds in the high mountain valleys each summer. Usually one man, with a horse and a good sheep dog, could handle four or five hundred sheep on a drive up into those valleys, keep the herd together for the summer while they ate the grass and drank the water, then drive them down to the main ranches in the Arkansas Valley come fall. Not a job I'd sign up to do, but, on the other hand, I know a lot of people who wouldn't give two cents to be a combination editor, writer, typesetter, ad salesman, and general handyman for a one-man weekly newspaper stuck way back in the mountains. So Cal Viner did his job and I did mine.

Viner handled the sheep like he'd had some experience. After that first season, he took a herd of sheep into the high country every summer. He wintered at the Ajax, one of the silver mines up in the high lonesome. It worked out fine for everybody: Viner wanted his privacy and the mine owners wanted a winter caretaker because the mine only operated in the summer months. One way or another, the only time we saw Viner in Buena Vista was when he came in to stock up on supplies.

Cal Viner was a loner all right. Still, we got to know one another over the next few years. He liked to take a drink now and then, play a little chess and cribbage, and talk—boy, did he like to talk! True, he was hard to get started. Usually he was one of those quiet ones that could sit for an hour and not say ten words, but when he got to drinking and philosophizing—the more drinking he did, the more he philosophized—nobody could hold a candle to him.

I used to like those sessions as much as he did. Sometimes he'd stop by the office when he was in town for supplies. Now and then I'd take a day off from the news-papering business. That's the nice thing about editing a country weekly: You can always shut things down for a while. When I'd get the chance, I liked to drive up to the high lonesome to have a drink, cook a dinner and spend some time around the campfire of Viner's sheep camp in the summer or his Ajax line shack in the winter. One place or the other, we drank a lot of whiskey and ate a lot of steak and beans. Cal became a good friend, although it took me a long time to figure him out. He liked to talk on those visits, but he didn't ever say much about himself. I always thought there was a story there to be told, but I had to wait a long time before I finally understood.

It was well into the 1980s, long after Viner was a familiar face around Buena Vista, that I finally got my story. Viner was still running sheep in the summers and had just settled into the line shack at the Ajax for another winter as caretaker when I drove up to see him. The fall color was early that year. The quakies high on the sides of the valley were already turning to brilliant reds and yellows, standing out sharply from the pine forests around them. As I bumped along the dirt road running higher and higher into the mountains, there was a nip in the air. All the signs were there for an early winter that year. The jeep was loaded with enough meat, fresh bread and whiskey to keep Viner and me fixed for a couple of days. I was ready for a little time in the high lonesome myself. Sometimes living in town can push—and push—until a man just needs to get away for a while.

The line shack at the Ajax was as high as high lonesome can get. It was perched high on one shoulder of the mountainous wall ringing the valley floor some eighteen hundred feet below. The Ajax was as far removed from civilization as you could get in Colorado. By the time I arrived at the shack the afternoon sun was still bright, but the approaching shadow of night had already filled the valley floor below. Even in the sunshine high on the mountain, the air was turning cold.

Cal was in the cabin doorway when I arrived. We unloaded the jeep, had a drink or two, and settled down on the front porch to watch the last of the sunlight disappearing to the west. He seemed especially glad to see me and we had a good evening, with a few more drinks and a good meal. After dinner we played a few hands of cribbage and then settled down by the open fire in the line shack.

Cal looked out the window. "It's beautiful out there, isn't it? We ought to remind ourselves every day just how beautiful this country really is.

"Have you ever lived anywhere else except up here in the mountains? Believe me, you don't know how lucky you are. I used to live north of New York City in one of those fancy commuter neighborhoods. Used to drive to the train station every morning just in time to catch a late, dirty train for the city, take the trip to Grand Central Station, and rush through the crowded, dirty streets to my office. Along the way I'd step over a few piles of trash, and sometimes even step over a few filthy rags and baggy old clothes containing some bum curled up on the street, like a fetus ready to depart life rather than arrive. It was a rare day when I wouldn't see a hooker, herself hooked on drugs, trying to ply her trade with some of the scummy characters on the street. Meanwhile, all the 'normal' people were on their way to work in that civil war of automobiles and pedestrians that constitutes New York traffic. Sometimes the sense of suffocation was overpowering. The newsstands displayed their sex magazines, the state-operated lottery windows sold their version of the numbers racket to the people who were too poor to pay the bill. The walls around me on the street were covered with graffiti. The panhandlers were on most every corner.

"If hell is where nobody has anything in common with anybody else except that they all hate one another and can't get an inch of space to be alone, then more and more of big city life has got to be some kind of hellish training ground, full of filth, impotence, agony, despair, terror.

"And don't think I'm just knocking the big city. Even when you get home to the suburbs you find that the main motive for action seems to be keeping up with the Joneses, who most of the time aren't even worth knowing, much less keeping up with. Sometimes I think that when we do anything just because other people do it, rather than because the thing is good or kind or honest in its own right, we've already lost our moral bearings.

"My nemesis at work was a man named Marcus Wimpsinger. This guy made even the Joneses look good. He was a perfect organization man, given to memoranda protecting his little behind, office gossip and a general standard of conduct totally at odds with his fellow man.

"There comes a moment when you begin to commit suicide a day at a time. You do the work but you retreat from life. You take care of everybody, but they don't really seem to touch you anymore. Then one day you decide that enough is enough. You walk away and tell yourself that you're taking back your dignity. But it isn't certain that you really can reacquire your dignity so easily. There are some difficult questions. The world is full of half-failures, but when you turn your back on those failures, are you reacting to enemies who should be cheerfully abandoned or are you reacting to incompetent friends, people to whom you have an obligation?

"We all owe a debt of gratitude to lots of people in our lives. The real question is how we go about paying back that kindness. There really isn't any way of measuring in terms of money what you owe some of those special people. You could pay them back forever and still be indebted to them. Besides, maybe they don't need any help or maybe they need a kind of help you can't give them. So the best you can do is look around for somebody that is in need of help and do what you can for them. Maybe all the debts eventually get cancelled out that way.

"Anyway, that's what I did. I walked away and left it all behind. The trouble is you can never really leave your life behind. When you walk away from things because of the negative effect they have on you, you seem to bring yourself, and therefore the negative effects, along with you. Only slaves and convicts and children can ever really run away successfully. Children can hide in their imagination. Convicts can tunnel into the stone walls and escape their ten-year sentence. Even slaves get a chance to go over the hill sooner or later. But when a free and consenting adult decides that he's going to run away, he finds that he's only running in a circle. What really bothered him about the failures in other people's lives will always continue to bother him as a failure in his own life.

"We're not free until we learn to help other people. It isn't enough just to say that the world is too bad off to be helped. I've had nearly ten good years of a way of life that I wouldn't trade for everything I saw in the big city and in my professional life. I wouldn't go back to anything in that way of life for a moment, but I have had a long time to think about it and I know that neither my life nor anyone's life is really worth living until you finally decide to do something for somebody else. The country can be beautiful, the company can be good, but that old pitiless, untiring dog-pack of remorse will always chase you no matter where you go. That failed opportunity dogs my steps or any man's steps until he finally pays his bill."

Cal Viner and I talked and drank long and hard that night. I never did get Cal to tell me exactly what job he thought he'd left unfinished, but it was obvious that that job, whatever it was, was still weighing heavily on him. The more we talked, the more clear it became that Cal was still looking for a way to repay an old debt that only he remembered.

"In the old days I used to think that I knew all the answers. I finally discovered that God doesn't give *all* the answers to anyone. He'll give you the clues—but it's up to you to find the answers. To hear people talk you'd think that they believe that God had decided to retire after His six days of Creation and had left men here to make up their own rules. He created human nature and this garden we play in rather like He was founding a nursery to give

His little spirits a chance to grow. Don't ever think that He isn't still tending the nursery. Life and everything in it is a gift. You're supposed to give as much of that gift to others as you possibly can. That's how this nursery works. That's how you grow.

"Real happiness is understanding that we're all in this together, that it is in giving that we escape our own prisons. Only a comrade can grasp our hand and haul us to freedom. When we pitch in to help someone who's in trouble, when we cry aloud in our own hour of need, then and then only do we learn that we are not alone. Then and then alone do we really come alive and fully sense the universe around us, the lights and beauties of our dear earth, the laughter and heartache of being human beings, the unending heroism of imperfect men reaching out toward perfection."

I asked Cal if he were speaking about a church, about some kind of religious experience, but he jumped all over me, insisting that the divine part of man was so elusive and impalpable that we couldn't embody it in the concrete form of a church or a social system. For him, the trip had to be made alone. The more we talked about the idea of a religious experience, the more angry he became.

"A man finally has to make his own choice and don't ever ask me to choose between the pirates and the preachers—I'll take the pirates every time. At least they don't presume to speak for God.

"Sanctimonious hypocrites! Do they really think they can speak for God? Do they really think they've been appointed to judge the rest of us? Look around you sometime, really look around. You see that God's work goes on with each of us—maybe we listen, maybe we don't. That's up to God, not His self-appointed judges on this earth.

"Judgment Day is really going to be something, isn't it? You know the best part? You and I—and everybody—are all going to be there, giving out with those puling little excuses:

It wasn't my fault, God. All those other people made me do it. You know me, God. I'm not like all those other people. They don't understand. You and I understand, God. All those dumb people! If only they had done their jobs; if only they had cared; if only they had really tried! I told them, Lord, why didn't they listen? I'd have helped more, too, Lord. But I had to be so careful. You can't have any influence in this world, you can't do God's work, if you offend the people who make things happen. Without the movers and shakers, without the people who make it happen, nobody can influence anything—not even God.

I'm sorry, God! I didn't mean that. You can do whatever You like, can't You? I'd have helped them more if I could—those other people were so stupid. They didn't know what You and I know, God. I know You told us not to judge one another, but what You must have *really* meant is not to judge the poor bastards on the same level as *we* can operate—I didn't mean *we* exactly. I know You're first, God, but You have to have Your representatives. Even God needs help, right?

Please forgive me, Lord! You don't need any help. You give and You need not receive. In Your mercy, protect me from the idiots, including the ultimate idiot—me.

"A prayer for all the smart-asses, especially me: May God protect us from ourselves. May we see the blessings all around us—the blessings of this day, the sunrise, the sunset, the friends, the loyalties, the faces of the little children—may we know the blessings of work, of sacrifice, of believing in something strongly enough to do our job, to live and if necessary to die, to do God's work.

"May we serve and please you in newness of life.

"Please give us that blessing—Your blessing. We ask it in Christ's name, Amen.

"I'm not sure what the Trinity means. None of us can truly know God the Father—at least not in this life. God the Son has promised always to be there—the bridge between God and man. And the Holy Ghost! I'm not sure I'm up to meeting Him—but He's met me every step of the way. Every time I *really* tried—to love someone, to do my job, to do what our Creator has every right to expect—the Holy Ghost was there giving me a push.

"I'm not talking about Baptists or Catholics; I'm not even talking about Christians or Jews. I'm talking about God.

"Dear God, I hope I have the courage to accept what You so freely offer."

Cal and I got pretty drunk that night. I'm not sure I followed everything he said and I'm not sure I've reported it accurately. But I'm sure that he had something on his mind so powerful that he couldn't let it rest.

I didn't see much more of Cal that winter—once or twice when he came to town. It seemed that he was a little embarrassed about that night and having laid bare his soul so very strongly. He wasn't mad at me, but he did seem all the more to want his privacy.

What happened at the Ajax the next spring, I know only second hand. The early work of reopening the mine for the summer was under way. Cal was still around camp and wouldn't be heading out into the Arkansas Valley to pick up his sheep for the summer for a few days yet. He was standing in the line shack door looking down the hill toward the mine when the cave-in occurred.

All hell broke loose as a branch off the main shaft collapsed, catching ten men below ground. Cal pitched in with the cook and the six miners who were still above ground. They were nearly forty miles from town and without a telephone, so anything that could be done had to be done fast, without any outside help.

The eight men battled for nearly three hours as they cleared the tunnel mouth a step at a time. For several hours they worked in a frenzy with no certain idea that the men within the mine were still alive. They worked under great peril themselves, because the tunnel they were clearing was still extremely shaky. The timbers were down and the entire opening might close again at any moment, trapping the rescuers as well.

About three o'clock that afternoon they finally penetrated the cave-in and reached the workers on the other side. The temporary rescue tunnel was small, scarcely wide enough to accommodate one man. Four of the miners had died in the cave-in, three more were severely injured. After the three healthy miners had wormed their way through the damp darkness of the crumbling opening, emerging blinking in the bright sunlight of the open tunnel, Cal was the first man to begin to worm his way back through to the three injured men.

The tunnel was groaning and shifting, about to fail at any moment. Cal crawled down the narrow shaft with a rope tied around his waist, reached the three men, and tied the rope under the arms of one of them. As the men outside the tunnel pulled on the rope, Cal wormed his way back through the tunnel, following the injured man, working him past rocks, ledges, and turns, as they moved toward open air and safety.

After the first injured man was safely out of the tunnel, Cal started in again despite the clear warnings that the tunnel might close at any moment. Again, he crawled the entire length of narrow, twisting darkness to reach the second man, adjust the rope around his body, tug on the rope for the group outside to begin to pull, and again work the man a few inches at a time through the long and tortuous route. Again, Cal and the second injured man reached safety.

By then, Cal was bloodied, covered with mud and exhausted. The entire crew was working in a frenzy of fear and exhaustion to reach the last man before the make-shift tunnel closed again. Another man started through the tunnel, with a rope tied around his waist, on his way to reach the third and last survivor. The shifting tunnel began to drop rock, closing the path just ahead of him. He slowly negotiated his way backward out of the tunnel, gasping for air. Without a word, Cal untied the rope from the man's waist, tied it around his own, and began the trip into the mountain. When he reached the place where the slide had occurred, he dug at the rocks with his bare hands until he'd opened a large enough path to force his body through. The long rope disappeared farther and farther into the darkness behind Cal. He reached the last man, attached the rope to his body, and tugged on the rope to ask the help of the miners in hauling the last casualty to safety. That tug was his last communication with the outside world. Cal and the last injured miner perished together when the tunnel collapsed in a crushing, suffocating roar.

There, in darkness and death, one man held his hand out to another in need.

I have never known what act in Cal's life caused him to feel such guilt and remorse. But I do believe that Cal Viner found peace. I like to think of that big quiet man now living in an even more beautiful world where a man holds his hand out to his neighbor in need.

# Things Used to
# Be Simpler

I'VE been the sheriff around here for a long time. I've watched times change and watched people come and go. When I first came here as a young man after World War II, things seemed a lot simpler than they are now. People took care of their own, worked for a living, generally minded their own business. Now it seems as though a lot of folks don't take care of their own, don't work for a living, and don't mind their own business. All those changes mean that there's a lot more for the government to do. Right here in this little mountain county we've got social workers and programs and counselors until hell won't have it. We used to laugh about all the silly things the folks in the big cities did—now we're doing the same things here.

Don't know what the world's coming to. Sometimes I'm glad my sheriffing days are about over. But once in a while I get to remembering some of the people I've known and I get kind of proud, proud of them, proud to have been a part of life up here in the mountains.

I remember a couple of old villains who ran a little ranch a few miles north of town, up toward Leadville where the mountains close in pretty tight on both sides of the Arkansas River, leaving precious little room for pasture or anything you might call ranch land. These old boys always made out all right, though. Maybe they were just too mean to give up. Like I said, the place wasn't much, but it was well tended and looked like somebody was working hard to keep things fixed up.

The ranch actually belonged to Arch McLennan, a tall, heavy-set man who'd retired after twenty years in the Navy and decided to find a ranch like the one where he'd grown up as a kid. Arch had been running the place since about 1930 and had long since become a part of the mountain valley where he lived and worked. He was the kind of a man that looked like he'd been hewed out of a chunk of granite. Friendly enough, but not one for much talk, Arch worked hard, minded his own business, and expected others to do the same. He had one of those faces that had taken the beating of a hard life, one of those proud faces that kept getting tougher with age.

For years after he first came, Arch was alone on the ranch. Then one summer he hooked up with an old ash-hauler from Pueblo. Hannigan was his last name, maybe his only name—I never heard anybody call him anything else. McLennan had gone to town for supplies one day and had stopped at the Green Parrot for a drink before going back to the ranch. Hannigan was up from Pueblo to get the steam baths out at the Hot Springs. He usually visited the valley for those sweats at about the same time each summer. The two of them had closed the Green Parrot a few times during Hannigan's summer visits in previous years.

Hannigan had cooked himself all day in the steam and the hot water, and had driven into Buena Vista to "put a few of the poisons back in my body." So there they were,

McLennan and Hannigan, sitting in the Green Parrot over a shot and a beer, discussing the state of the world with the genial proprietor, Dominic Belmonte. I'm glad I happened to be in town that day—sort of gives a feeling of having been in on things from the beginning.

Hannigan had a big, drooping gray mustache that mostly covered his mouth, although that sure didn't keep him from talking all the time. The mustache made him look older than McLennan, but I imagine that then, back in the mid-1940s, they were of an age, probably both in their early sixties. McLennan was clean-shaven, tall, straight, dignified. Hannigan was a head shorter, stooped, not too worried about being clean, and not too concerned what anybody thought about it.

With his second drink, Hannigan warmed to his subject. He scratched a big kitchen match on his boot and cupped the flame with a gnarled, big knuckled hand as he lit his blackened old pipe. "I've been cleaning out peoples' ashpits for damn near forty-five years and I think I'm gettin' ready to do something else. One reason is my daughter. I've been livin' with Sarah and her husband since my wife died. More than pay my way, but it seems my daughter don't like my table manners—always talkin' about gravy in my mustache. For my part, I never figured being fancy made food taste any better.

"I guess what tore things was one evening when we were sittin' around the living room, readin' and sewin', readin' and sewin', just like every other damn night. I asked 'em if they ever did anything different. Said the regular way they did things reminded me of a goddamn roomful of clocks. By the time we got through talking about that, it was time for me to be on the way for a few days to let things cool off. But to tell you the truth, I don't know if I want to go back this fall. I'm tired of hauling ashes and damn tired of livin' with my daughter and her husband."

I guess McLennan was tired of living alone out at that ranch too, because by the time that evening was over, Hannigan was on his way to McLennan's place to try his hand at ranching for awhile. Things must have worked out all right. Hannigan stayed right on into the winter. There's always plenty to do around a ranch, so an extra hand is nice. If the hand can play a little cribbage sitting by the fire at night, so much the better. Before that first winter was over, each man knew he'd found a friend he could trust to stand back to back with him against the whole damned world.

Late that winter a few of us from town went up to Granite for some Mexican food. On the way back we stopped by the ranch to see McLennan and Hannigan. McLennan welcomed us in out of the cold. We were just getting the snow shaken out of our Mackinaws when Hannigan came in, stamping snow from his boots and dropping a big armload of wood by the fire. "Damn these old feet of mine. They just can't stand the cold. If I'd known I was going to live this long, I'd have taken better care of myself."

McLennan had the whiskey out and we put a couple down. I said something about how most people can't seem to tell the difference between sense and nonsense. That was all it took to set Hannigan off. He lit his pipe, sucked a little leftover bread and gravy out of his mustache and settled down for his evening lecture.

"Most of us are inclined to think we know the difference between sense and nonsense. We actually believe that we think logical, consecutive thoughts. Not so, partners!

Most of the time we're just making noise or listening to other people's noise to hide how scared we are. If you don't believe in God, you can't believe in Heaven, if you don't believe in Heaven, you can't believe in life after death, and if you don't believe in life after death, death is all there is waiting for you. So they've got to keep shouting into the dark every minute, to keep death at arm's length, to keep from admitting how scared they are. That's why there's so much nonsense and so little sense being poured out in the world. If the dummies would shut up and listen for a minute, they'd hear God's voice and know there wasn't anything to be afraid of."

McLennan grinned, "See why I keep this old poop around? He's not as stupid as he looks."

It was about a year later, in the late 1940s, that McLennan's "family" grew again. A drifter came through Buena Vista looking for work. He was a good hand, but most people didn't want to sign him on because he was a lone man taking care of his little girl, about six years old. Mama had left the two of them somewhere down the line a couple of years before. McLennan and Hannigan decided to give the guy a chance. They weren't sorry. He worked hard, and besides, both those old villains loved that little girl from the start. By the end of the summer, they built another room on the house and asked the girl and her dad to stay on for the winter.

That kid, Allie, was a tomboy from the first. She was as tough as any youngster I ever saw. Never did cry. She took to big old McLennan and little Hannigan right away. They were always taking her to town on Saturday, picking her up at school in Buena Vista when she started first grade, wandering around the ranch telling her about this and that. It was a real love affair from the word go. I used to pin a deputy's badge on Allie and let her play sheriff in the office. Hannigan played "hello" with Allie at the ranch, walking around the barn and corral, touching different equipment or animals and saying their names. The little blonde girl would repeat the name: "hello, horse; hello, barn; hello truck." That was a game Allie never tired of, no matter how often they played.

The closest thing to trouble that first fall came up one day at the school in Buena Vista. McLennan arrived to pick up little Allie after school in time to hear some bigger girls teasing her about her clothes. There was also a part of the teasing that made fun of Allie because she didn't have a mama at home. McLennan didn't say a word, just offered Allie his big hand. They marched up the street to the mercantile store and got some new clothes that day. The proprietor thought it was kind of funny to see big old McLennan in there shopping for little girl's clothes. When the proprietor said something about it and snickered a little, McLennan stiffened slightly. Allie sensed it and touched him, murmuring in embarrassment, "Please don't have trouble because of me!"

McLennan looked the storekeeper right in the eye and said, "Trouble? There's not going to be any trouble, is there, mister?"

That ended Allie's troubles in Buena Vista. From then on, she was Allie from the McLennan Ranch, period.

The dad and both uncles all had to go out to the Hot Springs the day that Allie learned to swim. Nothing would do but that all three of them had to go in the pool and give her instructions. Everybody had a try, but it was finally the old navy man that saved the day. Allie was about in tears that day and none too sure about going in the water. McLennan picked her up in his arms, put her on the side of the pool and whispered in her ear, "Allie, to do something, first you've got to be something. Be confident, jump in, and the water is yours from then on. Once you get wet, clear to the top of your head, I can teach you to swim in ten minutes."

Allie jumped in and damned if he didn't teach her. Before it was all over that day, little Allie was swimming on her own. On the way home that night, the little girl fell asleep across McLennan's lap as the three men drove beneath the shadow of the mountains in the old pickup.

It was a little after Christmas that winter that everything changed. Allie's dad had taken a job at Climax working in the molybdenum mines to help generate a little extra money while things were slow at the ranch during the winter. A bad cave-in took his life the second week of work.

McLennan and Hannigan came to town to pick up Allie at school that day. I don't believe either of them ever did anything harder in their lives.

The next few days were tough for everybody. Nobody knew what kin Allie's dad might have. We buried him in the Buena Vista cemetery. I will say for the town that damn near all of them turned out for the services. Not that it made much difference to Allie. She stood there by her father's grave like a big girl throughout. Little Hannigan and big McLennan stood there like bookends, ready to fight the world for that child.

McLennan was fit to be tied for the next two weeks. Snapped the head off of anyone who tried to talk to him. Couldn't get him to take a drink. Said he had something to think through first.

One day he and Hannigan came into my office. McLennan had made up his mind. "We've got to try to find Allie's mother. We owe it to the child."

Hannigan was furious. He kept brushing down on that droopy mustache of his like it was full of ants. "Damn you, McLennan, we're Allie's kin now. We've got to take care of her. Besides, you blockhead, even you ought to know enough not to spurn the small gifts that come our way. They're always the most precious. Allie is a miracle in our lives. You can't throw that away!"

McLennan stood up. "Hannigan, the truth is the truth. All your jawing doesn't change it one damn bit. Allie has natural kin and we have an obligation to find her. That's the way it's going to be."

And that's the way it was. McLennan asked my help in using the Denver police to track down the mother. I didn't have any legal standing in Denver, but I went along with them as a friend. We were a pretty woebegone bunch. Allie didn't want to go, but McLennan had told the little girl we all thought she had to find her mother. Hannigan made lame jokes. McLennan sat beside Allie in the car, silent, staring straight ahead, his hand resting lightly on her blonde hair.

We finally found Allie's mama in a motel out on Santa Fe Drive. I had called about two hours before and she was supposed to be expecting us. When I saw the neighborhood, my heart sank. I was praying to God that Allie's mom and her situation wouldn't be as bad inside as it looked from the outside. McLennan and Hannigan were as grim as a trip to the gallows. McLennan and Allie went to the door of the motel unit. Some big guy in his undershirt opened the door, took one look, said over his shoulder, "Your kid's here," and turned back inside the room.

McLennan flushed as the screen door slammed in his face. He stood there, not saying a word, his big hand wrapped around Allie's. From inside we could all hear muttering sounds of talk, a man and a woman. The talk wasn't smooth or happy. It jabbed at the silence.

"Come on, Carl. I want to see my baby." The slurred sounds of a drunken woman's voice were too loud not to hear.

The woman appeared in the doorway, clad in a night-gown and mules, puffy and unkempt. As she opened the screen, the man in the undershirt grabbed her and spun her around. "No! The kid is going and she's going now."

McLennan stepped through the open doorway, thrust himself between the man and the woman, and shoved the man in the undershirt hard against the wall. "Don't you see that little girl standing there, mister?" McLennan's eyes burned with an unholy glint. The man in the under-shirt started to react and then backed off across the room. He didn't say a word.

The woman swayed in the middle of the room for an instant, her daughter looking up at her a few feet away. Then she rushed across the room to the man in the under-shirt. "Did he hurt you, Carl? I'm so sorry, I don't know what I was thinking of."

McLennan stood perfectly still for just a moment, then turned, grasped Allie's hand as he came out the door and said, "Come on, kid, we're going home."

We got out of Denver as fast as we could. At that stage I didn't know what the police or the juvenile people were going to do. I figured they could tell me about it later—much later—if they ever looked me up in Chaffee County.

It wasn't long before the Denver social workers were checking into Allie's whereabouts. Seems they thought that since her mother didn't want her, she ought to be in a juvenile home in Denver. I don't even remember what we did with the damn paperwork. That was nearly twenty years ago and things weren't nearly so complicated as they are these days. Anyway, we managed to keep Allie with us and nobody from Denver ever came looking for her. I don't think those guys in Denver ever did figure out what happened.

But Allie knew what happened. That little girl looked up at McLennan like he'd just saved her from hell. Maybe he had. I do know it all came out the way it should. Allie, McLennan, and Hannigan have had twenty years with their little family. That girl had two fathers and the most loving home you ever saw. Allie was the valedictorian at Buena Vista High School, went through Colorado State, and graduated as a veterinarian. She practices in Buena Vista, lives on the ranch, and has a couple of good-looking young bachelors who'd like to marry her. These prospective husbands had better be tough: McLennan and Hannigan are still living on the ranch. Coming in to pick up Allie and having to face those two old Buddhas could be a pretty scary experience for most youngsters, but I'm sure Allie can handle it.

As for those old villains, they're in their eighties now, still getting a fair amount of work done around the place and proud as hell of their beautiful blonde daughter.

Like I said, things used to be simpler.

# St. Elmo

THE dusty station wagon rolled to a stop in the front of St. Elmo's only business, a combination grocery store and filling station. It was an early afternoon in mid-June, but the sun was already dropping behind the great bank of mountains to the west, throwing a growing shadow across the valley floor.

The young couple and their ten-year-old son emerged stiffly from the car, stretching travel-weary arms and legs, looking around them at the tiny mining ghost town of St. Elmo. They were far back in a mountain valley surrounded by some of Colorado's wildest mountains, breathing the fresh clean air and the excitement of a new start in a new place.

The Andersons were city people. When the father, Jim, had an opportunity to quit his job as a factory worker in Denver and bring his family to a new start and a new life in the mountains operating a provisioning site for summer tourists and fall hunters, he jumped at the chance. His wife Kathy had not been too sure at first. Giving up a sure income and taking a chance living in the high lonesome seemed a little too romantic for her. The drive from Denver had taken the Andersons over a hundred miles into the mountains. After they left the main highway and drove up a dirt road for the final twenty miles through some of the most beautiful mountain country imaginable, the spirit of adventure had overtaken Kathy Anderson as well. The Anderson's young son, Tim, had required no urging from the beginning. Life in the mountains seemed to promise pure adventure to the ten-year-old.

Together the family poked around the abandoned town located on the end of such an unimproved dirt road that it hardly counted as a road at all. The town buildings were clapboard, weathered and gray after over half a century without paint, battered by the hard winters of the Colorado high country, yet still standing in dignified testimony to a generation long gone. The surrounding country rose sharply in all directions to form a great bowl of pine-covered slopes around the little mining town of long ago. The sound of the creek running down the valley floor a few feet north of the tiny ghost town provided the only sound to be heard except for a gentle sigh of the wind as it ran through the tops of the pine trees.

"Oh Jim, you were right! This place is beautiful."

The young husband stood with his arm around his wife as they breathed in the air and looked around their new home. Tim was already down by the water tossing rocks into his private stream.

"This is going to be home, Kathy. There will be plenty of business this summer and on through hunting season. You wait and see. We'll have enough before we're through to get us everything we need to go through this first winter. We'll clean up the store and add on to it gradually. We'll lay in more than enough wood and supplies for the winter. Tim can go to school down in the valley. This is going to be our home."

Even in June it gets dark early on the valley floors of the high country. The Andersons managed to clean up a small area in the front of the store. Using some of the wood they found in the corner, they soon had a fire going in the old potbellied stove. That first night they heated their dinner on top of the stove, eating the pork and beans on paper plates and mopping the sauce with slices of white bread. They had fresh water from the spring, sleeping bags from the car, and pack rats for company during the night. The next morning they were stiff and cold, but they soon had another fire going in the old stove, a coffee pot bubbling, and some bacon and eggs for breakfast. That day, work began in earnest. Cleaning, sweeping, repairing, discovering, the Andersons pitched in.

It wasn't until late that first full day that Tim came running back breathless with the news that one of the cabins on the western edge of St. Elmo, half-hidden by the trees, had smoke coming from the chimney. "Dad, I'm sure someone is there!"

Jim Anderson grinned, "Now who in the world would be living way up here?"

"You mean who would be crazy enough to do what we're doing, don't you?" Kathy laughed.

Jim stopped work. "Let's go take a look at these neighbors of ours."

The Andersons had picked up their small piece of property in the county seat by paying the back tax bill. If there were any neighbors to be had in the ghost town of St. Elmo, the county clerk in Salida hadn't mentioned it. Whether the county clerk had mentioned it or not, the Anderson family did indeed have neighbors. That afternoon for the first time they met the Starks, Tony and Miss Annabelle. The Starks, brother and sister, were both probably in their eighties. Tony was long and lanky with the easy grace of man who was used to taking care of himself in a difficult environment. He was as quiet as Annabelle was talkative. Tiny and feisty with snapping black eyes, she was a bundle of energy, opinions, and unsolicited history of St. Elmo and everyone who had ever lived there.

That night the Andersons joined the old couple for a simple dinner in their small cabin on the west edge of St. Elmo. If it was a shock to the Andersons to know that they had neighbors in this ghost town, it was even more of a shock to the Starks. Tony and Annabelle had lived in St. Elmo for seventy-five years, coming to the mining camp in its boom days during the 1870s. That night the Andersons learned something about St. Elmo and something about their new neighbors. The big mining claim in the valley had been the Mary Murphy Mine, but after the great silver producer was fully under way and people began arriving in the valley attracted by the first strike, other prospectors, other claims, and other mines soon began to appear. By the time Tony and Annabelle arrived as small children in the 1870s, coming to town with their parents, St. Elmo already had a population of over 2,000 people, a drugstore, two sawmills, an ore mill, three hotels, five restaurants, three general stores.

The town's fortunes went up and down depending on the price of silver and the amount of mining activity currently under way. But there was always enough activity, especially at the Mary Murphy, to keep the town of St. Elmo going. On that night and for many nights to come, Tony and Annabelle told the stories of St. Elmo and the Stark family.

Miss Annabelle had cooked in the boardinghouses,

served as the schoolteacher for some years, and had run the general store for a time. Tony had worked in the mines, done the hunting to provide the fresh meat for the boardinghouse, and worked with his sister in the general store.

"In those days, after our folks died, Annie and I used to live way up there on the side of the mountain, up toward the Mary Murphy. If you look real close, you can still see where the old cabin stands," Tony said, pointing to a ridge high above the valley floor.

By 1900, St. Elmo was fast failing and becoming a ghost town. The mining that had made the town live was passing from the scene and wouldn't be back for many years. When it did return, it would be a newer and more modern form of mining which no longer required the services of the tiny ghost town of St. Elmo.

"But why didn't you leave?" Kathy asked.

"Leave? Where would we have gone? Landsakes, child," said Miss Annabelle, "we came here when I was four and Tony was seven. We were in our mid-twenties in the year of the influenza epidemic that took our parents. We had never really lived anywhere else. We liked it here. Oh, we took a trip or two out to look around a little. It always seemed as though there were too many people. Things were too busy. And we sure never found any place as beautiful as our valley. Do you read the Bible, child? One of the Beatitudes says 'Blessed are the pure in heart: for they shall see God.' We know the world's just a dress rehearsal for things to come, but for us it always seemed as though God was right here somewhere, sort of like this was a little bit of heaven that hadn't been messed up the way most of the world is outside. I guess that's why we're still here."

And they were. Tony and Miss Annabelle could tell you just where the general store had been, the post office, the stage station, the blacksmith's shop, the saloons, and the jail. It was their town. And by that summer of 1950, they had been there for seventy-five years. The last fifty they had been largely alone, except for some occasional tourists and hunters. The Starks were friendly enough, but pretty noncommittal toward most visitors. With the Andersons it was different from the beginning. The Starks seemed genuinely glad that the young couple had come there to live and even more glad that young Tim was there to hear the stories of the past and talk about what Miss Annabelle called "important things."

That first summer and fall went by fast for the Andersons and even faster for Tim. There was much work to be done. Enough tourists and hunters came by that summer and fall to pay for the repairs and to stock the larder for the winter ahead.

Both the Andersons and especially Tim had plenty of opportunity to listen to stories about St. Elmo's past. Tony loved to spend time with the boy. Miss Annabelle said this was "peculiar." She said usually grown folks couldn't talk to the old man, but Tim could. Sitting on the front steps of the cabin, Tony would open his old knife and begin whittling long, curling shavings from the piece of wood he picked up by the stove. The shavings would fall from the blade until Tony would stop whittling and stare down at them for a moment. Then he would begin to talk, soft spoken and absentminded as if he were slightly out of focus with everything around him. Once he began to talk, he was likely to continue for a long while, letting the boy ask those endless questions of every ten-year-old.

"Tony, how could you stay when all the other people

left? Once the town died how could you stay all these years?"

"Son," Tony replied, "a town is a place where things happen, where people know their partners in the job of living. Once a place has really become a town, like St. Elmo was a town, it never stops. This town is full of memories. The shadows are all around you: the miners, the dance hall girls, the mule skinners, the bartenders, the families and the little kids, they're all here."

Tim heard all the stories: the hard winters when the entire community was sealed from the outside world in an impenetrable wall of snow for winter months on end, the tunnel cave-ins, the influenza epidemic, the great grizzly that Tony Stark killed one winter in a face-to-face encounter that almost cost him his life.

"Gee, Tony, you sure were lucky!"

The old man looked up with a start. "Luck? Surely you don't believe, son, that all the good times and all the bad times and all the courage and all the loving and helping and fighting are just something that happens in this life cause you do them on your own! It's not luck. Son, some things are meant to be. You and I are playing out a life where the circumstances show us the way. No, son, I take that back. It's not circumstances that show us the way. It's God Almighty. We don't make all these choices on our own. Remember that, boy."

"But, Tony, weren't you ever scared in all those things that happened to you—with the grizzly, the mines, the snow. Didn't you ever get scared?"

"Sure, son, I got scared lots of times. There's nothing wrong with being scared. What is wrong is backing away. When you get in that kind of spot, you just have to say, 'Well, I don't know how the hell I got in this fix, but I'm here, so I guess I'd better do something about it.' Once you decide that, the rest isn't so bad."

So Tim Anderson began to lead two lives. One, the active, busy life of a boy working with his parents to help establish themselves in a new existence, a world bounded by hard work, school, family meals, and the rules his mother and dad laid down; the other life, reaching out in imagination through the stories of an old man who remembered so much and so many who had gone before, who had known this country when it was truly wild. After the first few months of school that fall, those two lives began to merge in many small ways, ways so small that Tim himself never realized what was happening. That is, he didn't realize what was happening until one day in school when a picture in his fifth grade history book, a picture of pioneers in a covered wagon, suddenly came alive and he realized that those people were not just a picture, but had been real flesh and blood, people who ate and dressed and worked and sometimes were tired and sick, real people like the people who had become so real for the boy in Tony's stories of St. Elmo.

From then on, St. Elmo became more and more a magical place for the young boy. That first fall at school down in the valley, he couldn't wait for his Dad to pick him up in the station wagon and make the long trip each day back up the gulch to St. Elmo. Sometimes he had to stay with the teacher for several days at a time when the snow became so bad that it closed the entire upper valley. When the break in the weather would finally come and he could ride up the valley in the cab of the snowplow, Tim was as glad as any ten-year-old to see his folks, but he was always especially glad to be back in his magical St. Elmo. He was fortunate to have as his parents not only the loving members of a family, but also a young couple who understood the values and attitudes that had kept Tony and Miss Annabelle in St. Elmo for all those ghostly years. To the Andersons, Tony and Miss Annabelle were not "strange," but were hardy souls, loyal to a past that lived in them and would live in St. Elmo so long as they were alive.

The winter flew by for Tim. Before he knew it, it was late May, school was out for the year. The great drifts of snow covering the valley floor were melting. As the wild flowers and the kinnikinnick began to appear with the arrival of the first warm days, the spring runoff began. This high mountain valley channeled an enormous amount of water into its great collection basin, water destined to course down Chalk Creek into the Arkansas River some twenty miles away, running south and west across the country, racing toward its ultimate destination in the Mississippi River and finally in the Gulf of Mexico.

Spring had come, the air was sweet, the Anderson family adventure had been a success. The isolation had been an adjustment for everyone, but had soon changed from a sense of loneliness to a sense of healthy solitude and quiet. The family had worked harder, spent more time together, read more than ever before in their lives. Their elderly neighbors, Tony and Miss Annabelle, had become dear friends, purveyors of a past that still lived for them in the little ghost town.

Perhaps that's what made it so hard to accept the news which came with a letter postmarked in Denver. The federal Department of the Interior and the State Bureau of Water Management informed the Andersons that a water conservation project had been approved which would build a dam across the narrow mouth of the great mountain bowl in which they found themselves, a dam destined to fill that entire mountain valley with water to be used as a part of the complicated water exchange system between the eastern and western slopes of the Colorado Rockies.

The timetable was clear. Dam construction was slated for summer and fall of 1951. The winter of 1951-52 would once again gather great amounts of snow and ice in the valley. And the spring runoff of 1952, together with the springs rising on the valley floor, would rapidly fill the mountain bowl to a height well above the ground level where St. Elmo was built in the bottom of the basin. Within a year, St. Elmo would be far below the water level of a great man-made mountain reservoir.

As all such letters do, this official communication from the government made it clear that "proper compensation" would be made to the Anderson family for the property which appeared in their name on the tax rolls at the county seat. No real choice or alternative was offered, no appeal process was available. Even if they stayed out the maximum time, the Anderson family was within a year of watching their new home disappear under the water.

The Anderson family walked slowly up the street, moving as though in shock. They were heading straight toward the little cabin on the west edge of St. Elmo. When they arrived, they found Tony and Miss Annabelle sitting on the front porch. Miss Annabelle was holding their government letter in her lap. The two of them said not a word. It seemed as though they simply could not digest the meaning of the letter bearing that Denver postmark.

There was a lot of talk that summer as the only residents of St. Elmo, indeed the only residents of that entire valley, gradually came to understand the meaning which the reclamation project had for them. Before summer was over, the Andersons had accepted the government offer, arranged a mortgage to purchase a small sporting goods store in Salida, the county seat some forty miles away, and were preparing to move to town in time for Tim to start school that fall.

The Starks were a different story. They had decided not to go.

"But you can't decide not to go!" Kathy urged. "You've got to go. By next summer this valley will be filled with water. Why do you want to stay?"

Miss Annabelle stopped rocking, took off her glasses, and polished them gently on her apron. "Dear, I like the silence. When it's really quiet, you have time to hear yourself think. You have time to decide what's important. That's what's the matter with the world: they are so busy fleeing silence that they never stop to think about what's really important. I guess they just prefer confusion. Well, I don't prefer confusion. I like to see the stars at night. I don't suppose it will be too long until I'm out there wandering around somewhere among those stars. There comes a time when you know you've already lived your life and that the rest is a kind of malingering. Tony and I have been here too long to do anything else, except prepare to meet our Maker in the one place where we always came closest to finding Him."

Little Tim spoke up from the cabin steps where he had been sitting, listening to the grown-ups talk. "But Miss Annabelle, you've got to go."

"Oh no I don't. People always have a choice about what they're going to do. The world can take most everything from you, but it can never take from you the freedom to choose what your attitude is going to be, to choose your own way. Tony and I may not be much at this stage in our lives, but we know who we are and we won't be robbed of it. We still have a choice and we'll have that choice so long as we're alive."

Construction of the dam had been going on some distance downstream from St. Elmo, closing the mouth of the great mountain bowl at its narrowest point. On their monthly trip to town for the few odds and ends which constituted their very simple needs, Tony and Miss Annabelle always looked straight ahead as their old Model A Ford bumped down the little dirt road past the construction site. It was as though the dam and its ultimate meaning simply did not exist for them.

It was mid-August before the world finally intruded. As usual, Tim Anderson was sitting visiting with Tony and Miss Annabelle when the sheriff's car arrived at the foot of the hill below the Stark cabin. The sheriff climbed slowly out of his car, as though he were somehow suddenly tired, or perhaps unwilling to face an unpleasant necessity. "Hi, Miss Annabelle. Hi, Tony. You're getting the royal treatment today. Like to have you meet the head man of this dam project. He wanted to come up and see you himself."

The engineer was a big, hearty man. There was no trace of his being ill at ease. "Good afternoon, Miss Stark, Mr. Stark. I know you received a letter from us some time ago explaining the project and our offer to buy your land. I thought perhaps the whole thing might have been a little confusing for you. Since we hadn't heard from you, I thought perhaps I could come up and explain what this is all about."

Miss Annabelle stirred in her chair. "We know what it's all about. You're trying to take our home."

"Now, now Miss Stark. You've got to understand that this is a reclamation project which will provide water for thousands of people as we develop Colorado into the state with a great future."

Neither Tony nor Miss Annabelle moved or spoke. The engineer fumbled for just a moment, cleared his throat and pressed on. "We're so sure that this is the right thing for you to do that we've even doubled the last price we offered you. A check in that amount has already been placed in the Salida bank. It's there in your name anytime you want to collect it."

Tony and Miss Annabelle sat there quietly on the porch looking straight at the engineer and saying nothing. The silence grew heavier and heavier. Finally the sheriff blurted out, "Damn it, I told you it wasn't going to do any good to come up here. Now go ahead and tell them the rest of it."

"All right, I will," snarled the engineer. "As a matter of fact, Mr. Stark, Miss Stark, this land has already been condemned. It belongs to the reclamation project now. We've come up here today to tell you to take your belongings and move to town and what you do after that is of no interest to me."

Still without saying a word, Tony rose slowly to his feet, stepped inside the cabin and returned a moment later with a .30-'06 in his hand. He levered a shell into the chamber, holding the rifle loosely in his hands as he looked the engineer directly in the eye and said, "Get off my land."

The engineer said, "This is no longer your land."

"I won't tell you again." Tony Stark's gaze never wavered from the engineer's eyes.

The sheriff stepped between the two men. Addressing

the engineer he said, "Damn it, I told you. Now get back in the car before I have to carry you."

As the engineer withdrew, the sheriff turned to Tony and spoke in a tired, old voice, "Tony, what the hell's the matter with you? You're dealing with the law now and if you're not careful, you're going to be in jail."

Tony shrugged, "Can't talk to that damn blow-hard."

The sheriff sighed, "Tony, you and Miss Annabelle are too old to be living up here alone. Isn't it about time for the two of you to move to town and take things a little easier?"

Tony shrugged again, "Never asked for anything to be easy. Just want to be left alone."

The engineer's voice boomed up the hill, "Don't those old fools know that next summer this cabin is going to be on the bottom of a lake? Enough is enough, Sheriff. Are you going to do your job and get them out of here?"

The sheriff turned and walked toward the car. "No, I'm not. I guess I'm an old fool, too. And if you say one more goddamn word to me, you can walk back to town."

The sheriff was back the next day, alone. "Tony and Miss Annabelle, I've done all I can. I'll let you stay through the winter, but you've got to be out of here before the water rises next summer. Reckon that can't hurt much."

Miss Annabelle spoke up. "You're a good boy, Jim. I knew your mother and dad. They used to come here when you were a little shaver, must be forty years ago. You were a good boy then and you're a good boy now."

The sheriff walked down the hill to return to his car. As he opened the door, he turned and looked back up the hill at the old couple on the cabin porch. "Remember now, you've got to be out of here before the water starts rising next summer. When I come back next time, you've got to come out with me."

The Anderson family was off to town soon thereafter. It was time to go to work with their small sporting goods store and time for Tim to start in his new school. Tony and Annabelle wished them well and the old couple obviously felt a sense of loss as their new neighbors left St. Elmo.

Miss Annabelle spoke as they were loading the car, "You take care of that boy now, you hear? And Tim, you take care of your folks. I don't want to hear any bad reports."

There are only two sorts of faces in the world—those that show everything happening to them and those that show nothing. Miss Annabelle was one of the second kind. There was no intimation of strain, no pressure which came through in her kindly old face. She was the same Miss Annabelle that the Andersons and Tim had discovered when they first came to the valley. That's why the telephone call was such a surprise when they heard Tony's voice over the static-filled party line that served the few telephones in the gulch. Tony had driven down the valley nearly ten miles to the first house with a phone and had called the Andersons with the news that Annabelle was seriously ill. She had suddenly collapsed while cooking breakfast and although she was now resting well, she seemed terribly pale and weak. Did the Andersons know a doctor well enough to ask him to come up the gulch to look at her?

Jim and Kathy Anderson did know a doctor and came immediately. After the doctor listened to Miss Annabelle's heart, he took Tony and the Andersons aside, warning, "Her heart is about to quit. This might happen at any time. I don't know that it will help to take her to the hospital, but if we can get her there we might be able to keep her going a while with oxygen and some intravenous feeding. I can't do much else here. If we handle it carefully in the car, I believe we can get her to town safely."

Tony stared straight ahead, as though he had no reaction or knowledge of the doctor's words. He offered no resistance or help as they prepared Miss Annabelle for the trip to town. On the way, he held Miss Annabelle's head quietly in his lap in the back seat.

Miss Annabelle was made of sterner stuff than the doctor realized. She grew stronger for the next few days and actually was to the point where she was again able to speak. It was late on the afternoon of the third day in the hospital when Miss Annabelle talked to her two favorite visitors, her brother Tony and her young friend Tim Anderson. The doctor had already warned that the heart damage was so severe that she might go at any time, but nothing in Miss Annabelle's tone gave any credence to such a suggestion.

"I wonder what difference it makes *when* you meet your Maker. Probably it's always too soon, and I suppose it's always too late as well. I suppose none of us can do much about the time when we go, but at least we can count ourselves lucky if we get a chance to say good-bye to our friends and our loved ones. A lot of people don't get a chance to tell their folks how much they love them. So get your mournful looks off your face. Tony Stark, you got to be the one that takes care of Tim from now on—at least help his folks do the job. And as for you, Tim Anderson, somebody's got to take care of Tony. I've been doing it for nearly eighty years and the good Lord knows he sure can't do it himself. Remember, both of you, God gives us an escape clause, a chance to know when enough is enough. When it's time to go home, it's time to go home. That's not grounds for sadness. That's grounds for happiness."

That night as Miss Annabelle lay alone in the Salida hospital room, she wondered about Tony. How would he hold up? How many more springs and how many autumns would he live without her there? That was the last question which Miss Annabelle had an opportunity to ask herself.

Tony Stark seemed completely lost with the funeral arrangements, the paperwork, and the visits of well-wishers. Jim and Kathy Anderson did most of the work in making the arrangements. The one thing on which Tony insisted, the one thing which would never have happened without the help of the Andersons, was the decision to bury Miss Annabelle high on the rim of the great mountain bowl overlooking St. Elmo, next to the little cabin which they had shared so many years before.

"Can't bury Annie down where our cabin is now. That's going to be under water pretty soon. Besides, I think Annie would like to be way up on the hill where we used to live in that old mining shack, kind of looking down on the valley and remembering all the people that came and went over the years."

Jim Anderson and the sheriff rounded up a few able-bodied men who managed to struggle with Miss Annabelle's coffin until they made it up the hill from St. Elmo that cold fall day. Winter was already in the air and it looked like it might snow before Miss Annabelle was finally buried beside her little cabin high on the mountain. The grave was dug, the casket was lowered, the small stone was erected, and Miss Annabelle was laid to rest.

Jim Anderson, the sheriff, and the others retreated a few feet down the hill as Tony stood beside his sister's grave and looked out over the valley, "I never thought I'd still be here when you were gone, Annie. But like you always said, man proposes and God disposes. I guess our job is just to do the best we can as long as we can. Hope you like it up here looking out over the valley. At least those damn reclamation people can't flood you out. I'll be back to see you as often as I can get up the hill. And, God willing, I'll be up here with you pretty soon. God bless you, sweetheart."

Jim and Kathy Anderson, and especially Tim, kept after old Tony to come down and join them for Christmas. He did. At their continued urging, he even stayed in town on through January, February, and March. As April and spring came to the Colorado Rockies, the old man was obviously beginning to get edgy. Sometimes he would walk to school to meet Tim when class was over for the day. When the spring sun was warm enough in mid-afternoon, the old man and the boy would sometimes stop on the way home and soak up a little of that warming sun on a park bench on one of the streets in the little town. Salida was a sleepy little county seat by the standards of most Americans in 1952, but it was a busy place for old Tony—too many cars, too many people, too many things going on. "Makes a man tired just watching."

On one of those afternoons, Tony was trying to tell his young friend it was time for him to go back to St. Elmo.

"But why, Tony? We love you. We want you here."

"Tim, a man has to do what he has to do. It doesn't really make any difference what we expect from life, but it makes a lot of difference what life expects from us. I don't think anybody can be happy unless we know what it is

130

we're supposed to be doing with our life. And I'm a stranger here, son. I don't understand life in town, I don't understand the people. The one thing I do understand is that Annie's in St. Elmo. My home has always been in St. Elmo, and it's time for me to go home. You know, some of these people in town think I'm crazy. But I'll tell you the truth, Tim, I *know* they're crazy."

The snow still stood in great banks on the hillsides and the valley floor. It was melting rapidly as spring turned to summer and Tony Stark returned home. The Andersons and Tim brought Tony back to his cabin on the valley floor, set up housekeeping with the supplies they brought from town, and even stayed overnight with him before they had to return to the store. As they left for the return trip to town the next day, Jim Anderson told Tony once again, "The water is going to be rising fast this summer. This whole place is going to be gone soon. When that time comes and you have to leave, remember you always have a home with us."

Tony thanked them in his quiet way and raised an arm to wave farewell as the station wagon started back down the valley. In the distance as he looked down the valley, behind the completed dam, he could see the stream already spreading, spilling out of its banks and beginning to form a growing pool of water. The spring runoff would soon be making that pool larger and larger as it crept closer to St. Elmo.

As it grew dark that night, Tony stood in front of the little cabin on the west edge of St. Elmo, took a deep breath of the cool air of the approaching night and looked up the mountain toward the little mining shack where Miss Annabelle was buried. "They're all gone now, but we're still here, aren't we Annie?"

That night Tony Stark sat by the fire and talked to himself until he was clear talked out. He watched the moon rise above the mountain wall and shine down through the pine trees on the valley floor. The moon was almost full. Tony could see the growing pond below the town as the water rose higher and higher in its slow, inexorable march.

The next morning the water was hot on the stove. Tony sloshed a little in the pan while he did a few dishes. He flipped that water out the front door of the cabin and brought the pan back for a refill, rubbing his hand gently over his chin and feeling the stubble. He found his old straight edge and shaving brush, propped his small piece of mirror on a shelf before him, and set about the task of shaving. "Wonder how much time I've spent shaving in the last eighty years. A lot of damn foolishness, but I've got to get cleaned up to go see Annie."

After the shave, Tony donned a fresh cotton workshirt and a clean pair of jeans, combed his hair, slipped on a jacket, and started up the hill. The light of a beautiful summer morning in the high country filled his eyes. It seemed as though he could see for miles—so clearly, so far. He felt fresh, strong, alive. Somehow this seemed as though it were his first day in the valley. He was a young man again, taken back in time to another, simpler world. Several times on his way up the side of the mountain toward the little mining shack, Tony stopped to look at the untouched wilderness around him. The valley floor lay far below him, the pines and the rocks spread in a private splendor touched only by the wind. The sun was warm on his face. As he paused to look over the valley, the thought came to his mind, "It's a little easier to breathe up

here. There's not so many people crowding a man's el-
bows." As that thought came to him, Tony looked downstream. From his position high on the hill, he could see
the dam clearly and the great spreading pond of water
moving up the valley toward St. Elmo.

When he arrived at the cabin high on the mountain
side, waiting for his old heart to subside in its rest after the
exhausting climb, Tony deliberately turned his back on
the dam and the great, growing pond of water. "Just like it
used to be, Annie. Just you and me."

As he sat there that day, the old man traveled back in
time. Suddenly he was seven years old, Annie was four.
He was coming home from his first day in the schoolhouse
in the mining town of St. Elmo. There to greet him as he
approached his family's cabin was little Annie, still a
baby, dragging a little straw doll by one foot behind her,
suddenly seeing her brother coming, dropping the doll
and rushing to meet him, her fat little baby arms out-
spread for love and for balance. He caught the little child
and held her in his arms.

It was a long day of memories. Suddenly it was late
afternoon. The old man woke from his reverie with a start,
looking about him as though uncertain where he was.

"Got to go now, Annie." He looked down at the stone at
his sister's graveside and read the inscription which she
had requested: "We must seek God alone, but we will
reach Him together."

The summer rushed by, the water rose. Already the
buildings on the downstream side of St. Elmo were more
than half under water. The great, shining surface of water
ate more and more of the valley floor, engulfing St. Elmo.

The Andersons came by when they could. Tim stayed

over a weekend several times that summer. The sheriff came by now and then to check on Tony and remind him that fall was coming and the water was rising.

Tony sat on his porch and watched the water rise. It lapped on his doorstep now. Most of the buildings closer to the creek were already under water. The rising tide explored each building, room by room, slithering on its way toward higher and higher ground. The day came when Tony awoke to see the water creeping under his front door, spreading across the floor of the cabin. As September became October, he moved his sleeping bag and his provisions up to the old mining shack on the mountain where Miss Annabelle lay buried. He patched things up enough to make everything livable for a while, at least until real winter weather came. There he watched as the weather turned cold and the last of St. Elmo vanished beneath the surface. One day the old man sat staring across the valley, watching the first skiff of ice form on the great lake below. He watched Jim Anderson, Tim, and the sheriff climb around the edge of the mountain, coming the hard way because the roads on the valley floor were now under water.

The sheriff stood by the old man's side. "Time to go home now, Tony."

"I'd like to stay the weekend. I promise that's the end. First, I'd like to spend the last day or two here with Annie."

Jim Anderson replied, "Well, we brought enough food from town to take care of you for another weekend. You sure you're going to be all right? I guess we could come back Sunday, but that's really got to be the end. The way things are going, we might have a big snowstorm anytime and there won't be any way to get in here."

Tim spoke up, "Dad, may I stay here with Tony?"

"No, you may not!"

Tony looked up. "I'd be glad to have the boy stay if he promised to be quiet. In fact, I'd kind of like the company. I think Annie would like to have Tim here too if it's all right with you."

Jim Anderson looked at the sheriff and frowned. "I don't like the look of the weather."

"Please, Dad, it's only October. Everything will be fine. Please, Dad, this is the last time we can ever be here at St. Elmo."

Jim Anderson looked at the sheriff, who looked back and shrugged. "Oh, all right. But I expect to find both of you here Sunday afternoon, ready to go to town."

It was back in town the next morning that Jim Anderson realized what a great mistake he had made. The snow had indeed come during the night, not the few flakes or brief squalls of October, but the great drifting, heavy snow of December or January. It had started sometime during the night after they were back in bed in Salida and it had continued ever since. By the time the Andersons were up in the morning, the sheriff had already arrived at their house. He had his big sheepskin coat, his jeep, two other men—and was ready to go. "This has been getting worse all night, Jim. They could be snowed in there for two weeks. Even if this lets up, we're going to have a tough time getting around the shoulder of that mountain in all this snow. The roads are long gone under the reservoir."

Four men were on their way to the valley within a few minutes. The twenty-mile trip along the highway had not yet been plowed and was tough enough. They would not have been able to make it that far without four-wheel drive. The next twenty miles up the valley toward St.

Elmo were nearly impassable. They spent most of the day in the effort, fighting every step of the way, digging themselves out of snowbank after snowbank, grueling mile after mile.

The snow had not stopped all day and was already approaching record levels. The air was filled with blinding white, the pine trees sagged under their heavy load. The drifts were to the point where not even the jeep could make it any farther.

The four men struggled up the valley on foot, but darkness overtook them still some four weary miles from the little mining shack on the side of the mountain.

"We've got to stop here, Jim. We'll lose our way in the dark. This is going to be tough enough in the light of day tomorrow," the sheriff warned.

The four exhausted men stood by a line shack several miles downstream from the dam, fully four to five miles from the mining shack high on the mountain side. Their breath hung in the frosty air around them as they huddled together in the blinding white darkness.

"Sheriff, I've got to go on. My boy is up there."

"Jim, you know as well as I do that all you'll do is go out and die in the snow tonight. Let's hole up in this line shack, get a little rest and have another go when the light's up. We'll never make it tonight and you know it."

The four struggled to light a fire, provide a little temporary shelter and get some nourishment in their exhausted bodies. The snow continued to fall—heavy, wet, blinding.

The next morning they were off again, fighting through drifts nearly chest high. The snow let up near midday and the sky turned clear and blue as it will after a Colorado winter storm in the mountains. With the sunshine the visibility was better, but the going was still almost impossible. It was mid-afternoon before they reached the mining shack. Ahead of the men across the edge of the mountain rim was the little shack, looking like a picture postcard as it nestled in the snow with a billowing cloud of smoke lazily rising from the chimney.

Tim saw them coming before they reached the cabin. "Dad! Dad! Dad!"

"Thank God you're all right, son." Jim Anderson took his son in his arms.

The sheriff stepped toward the shack. "How's Tony?"

The boy turned toward the shack where the sheriff stood in the doorway. "Oh don't wake Tony, he's awful tired. He's been sleeping all day. When the storm started, Tony knew we were going to need firewood and he went out and started chopping. He chopped and chopped and chopped for about five hours until it got too dark to see anything out there in the snow. He said we were going to need plenty of dry wood to hole up until you got here. When he came in and sat down, he told me to keep the fire going, stay inside and be sparing on the food that I ate. I tried to get him to eat something, but he said that we'd need it worse later, and besides he wasn't very hungry. He laid down and went to sleep right after that and has been sleeping ever since. He told me to stay inside, keep that fire built up and wait until you came. He kept telling me that under no circumstances should I go outside the cabin until you got here. Are you going to wake him now?"

The sheriff was standing by the old man's cot. "No, I don't think we'll wake him just now, Tim. He's been working pretty hard and I think he needs his rest. Jim, can I see you outside for a moment?

"Jim, the old man is dead. He was so busy trying to take

137

care of that boy and get some firewood up here that he finally just gave up the ghost. We're going to have to stay the night here before we try to break trail out in the morning. It's just too late to make a start now. I kind of figured that there's one thing we should do since we have a few hours of daylight left. There's no sense in taking Tony out of here. Let's get to work and clear away those drifts by Miss Annabelle's grave and dig a spot for Tony."

Well, that's how it was. The next day they broke trail out to the jeep and worked their way back down the valley and back to town. Tony and Miss Annabelle lie side by side, looking over their valley and St. Elmo far below.

# Ground Blizzard

I T was Christmas Eve in Fairplay. The darkness of a cold winter evening had descended on the little mountain town. The lights were coming on as people made their way home to a warm fire, a dinner with the family and some Christmas cheer. It was going to be a good night to be indoors. The wind was coming up, sweeping clouds of snow and tiny particles of ice before it in a blinding, suffocating blast.

The wind in Fairplay was in a class by itself. The little town was located in almost the exact center of a long, narrow valley, ten thousand feet above sea level and ringed by towering mountains. When the wind blew and the temperature dropped, it was time to be inside with the family, especially on Christmas Eve.

As Doc Oliver made his way down the street, leaning forward into the very teeth of the wind to make progress, the Christmas decorations strung across the main street were jangling crazily as the wind threatened to blow them away. The dark, the cold, and the snow made the lights of the Fairplay Hotel an attractive haven just a few feet farther ahead. Doc reached the hotel and stepped inside, accompanied by a great swirl of snow and cold. The walk from his home had been less than three city blocks, but he was already encrusted from head to foot. As Doc stepped through the hotel lobby and into the bar, shaking the snow and ice from his long, heavy coat, the bartender looked up from the newspaper he had been reading, "Some night, huh Doc?"

Doc hung his coat on the rack in the corner. "You can bet your life on that, Charley! It isn't fit for man or beast out there tonight. Where is everybody?"

"Home with their families where they belong, I guess. It's Christmas Eve, Doc. If I had anything better to do myself, I'd be doing it. There's not a soul staying here in the Hotel. Nobody's going to be out tonight. I already sent the cook home. Tell you the truth, Doc, I'm glad I have a room in the back. I'd hate to have to go out tonight."

Doc Oliver was a tall, thin man in his middle fifties. He had been a country doctor in Fairplay, the town's only doctor, for over thirty years. His hair was silver, his eyes were tired and he was glad to be in out of the snow. Doc looked across the bar, "Can I buy you a drink, Charley?"

"You can buy me a drink as soon as I buy you one, Doc."

The bartender poured out two shot glasses of whiskey and drew two beers from the tap. Charley knew his customer well. He had been running the Fairplay Hotel almost as long as Doc had been practicing medicine in town. A short thick man in his mid-sixties, Charley was a friendly soul who always had time for his friends, especially Doc. "I'm glad you came in, Doc. Another ten minutes and I was getting ready to turn the lights off for the night. Between the weather and Christmas Eve, I think you and I are about all the company we're going to have."

The next two hours went by fast for the two old friends. They stopped drinking and talking after a time and adjourned to the hotel kitchen to fix something to eat. They ate steak and potato chips as the wind roared around the hotel and the temperature dropped. Doc raised his beer and proposed a toast, "For Jack, John, Rusty, Ron, and all the rest, wherever they are on the earth, or under it. Here's to our friends!

"And now another toast, Charley, a toast for our kids. Attention, teenagers and young adults everywhere: If you're tired of being hassled by unreasonable parents, now is the time for action. Leave home and start paying your own way while you still know everything."

Charley looked up from his drink. "Now, Doc, it sounds like your talking about Gregory again. Your boy is gone—it's time to forget it. Besides, he'll be back when he finds himself. Hell, I'll bet you weren't any prize when you were twenty yourself. Kids have to grow up. Other people, especially your folks, can do a lot, but they can't tell you who you really are. A kid has to do that for himself."

Doc turned on his kitchen stool and looked out the window at the blinding storm of white, roaring by on the night wind. "Find himself! When do you find yourself? Do you ever find yourself? I'm not sure I ever did. Most of the things I thought were important haven't turned out to mean much. And the things I never gave a damn about are the ones that mattered, the ones I'd like another chance at. Besides, a lot of those ninnies out there 'finding themselves' are never going to grow up. A boy doesn't get to be a man until he has a man's job to do. The world is full of fifty-year-old boys because they never found anything to do that was important enough to require a man."

"Greg will be all right, Doc. A man has to take that first step and it was time for the boy to take his. He'll be gone for a while, but he'll come back to you. What's more, he'll come back a man. Give the boy a chance. Give yourself a chance. I saw Greg before he left town last summer. He loves you more than anything in the world, Doc. He promised me he was coming back. Said he wanted to make you proud of him and he had to go find the right place to do it. Doc, when a man makes a promise to do something, he's really making an appointment with himself. Your son made that appointment—and he'll be back. Meanwhile, let's wash these dishes and go back in the bar. The sound of that wind is getting into my bones."

Later, sitting on one side of the bar while the bartender leaned forward from the other side, Doc Oliver played with his drink and said, "Charley, you're probably right. Maybe my son did have to leave this town. I guess you've always got to reach out, to get past the place where you are. None of us can stand still too long. A man can't hold on too long. Sooner or later your baggage gets too heavy. If you're not growing and finding and loving, then you're dying. I've spent my life trying to keep things together— my family, this little town—and Charley, it doesn't work. One day you find yourself defending the indefensible. One day you find you're indefensible yourself. You get to be a caricature of the flesh and blood and love and courage that you and your ideas used to be.

"They say that good always triumphs over evil. Not so—left on the same level, with good always trying to meet evil on its own terms, evil eventually wears down good, brings it down to its own methods. The only good that wins out in the end is the good that finally remembers its source. You've got to rise above the evil. Evil touches us all, all except God. Until we find ourselves in His arms, being a 'good man' just isn't enough."

"That's right enough," Charley answered. "The trouble is that when we say such things we ought to remember that God may call in the chit—He may expect us to put up or shut up."

Doc polished the mahogany bar top with the sleeve of his sweater. "I know, I know—it's brave talk to tell everybody about doing God's work. Still, it makes me mad to listen to people telling one another that it wasn't their fault. No, it's always all those other people who are to blame. Charley, when you get right down to it, why should we care whose fault it is? For the love of God, don't we owe more than that to one another?"

Charley poured another round. It was growing late and the storm outside howled undiminished. "Doc, you've lost a wife for good and a son for a while. That doesn't mean you've failed. What you do really matters, even when things don't always work out. When you try your best, it really matters. Sometimes the failures and the bad days are a part of the truth, too."

Doc Oliver tossed off his shot and washed it down with a swallow of beer. "God knows, I've had my share of failures: A son gone, a wife who died hating my guts. You leave for work some morning, business as usual. Your wife steps into the car to go shopping in Denver—next thing you know, the Highway Patrol tells you she's never coming back. Just like that, someone gone after thirty years. Somehow it just makes it worse that we could never get along. I guess I'm just feeling guilty. I should have helped her more. She never was very strong. As she got older, it seemed she became more selfish, more afraid, more resentful. She needed so much help. Somehow I should have *made* her do more for her family, *made* her take part in living, in doing her job. I guess I just made life too easy: too much money, too many cars, too many shopping trips, too little work for her home and family. You call it 'kindness' when you're doing it, but it's really only neglect. I had my work. She didn't have much of anything. Hell, I was so busy saving the world that I never saw what was really happening."

The old friends sat in silence. "You know, Charley, maybe that poor, spoiled mess of a human being was Christ, maybe that's who I should have helped, and I just didn't see it. The cost of loving is very high, Charley, but the cost of *not* loving is a whole lot higher."

"Doc, it's been a hard year, but it's over now. Time to think about other things."

"I wish I could, Charley. They say you can live with almost any *how* in life so long as you have a good *why*. But Charley, I've forgotten the *why!* I don't know of anything that's worth doing. And I know one thing for damn sure, going back to that empty house tonight isn't worth doing!"

Charley drained his beer. "We're all trying to go home, Doc. Sometimes it's hard to find the way."

Doc Oliver stood up as though he had suddenly made up his mind. "I don't think I will go home tonight. Hell, it doesn't make any difference. There's nobody there—it's not home anymore."

The bartender tried to get Doc to stay at the hotel for the night, but there was no stopping him. He wrapped up in his huge coat, fur hat, muffler and gloves and, with a final "Merry Christmas," he was out the door and into the ground blizzard.

As he struggled toward his house in the blasts of blinding, stinging snow, the only half-acknowledged idea came to him that he didn't really care whether he got home or not. The idea took form that he ought to go to Denver for Christmas: stay at the Brown Palace, eat at the Navarre, see a few friends—anything but go back to that empty house that was waiting for him. The danger of the storm hardly entered his consciousness. When Doc arrived home, he went straight to the garage, started the car, and backed out into the storm. He was eighty miles from Denver over mountain roads, driving into the teeth of a ferocious mountain ground blizzard that reduced visibility to nearly zero, producing a wind-chill factor thirty degrees below freezing. Doc made his way slowly down to the main highway. It was after midnight. No other cars were on the road. As he turned onto the highway outside Fairplay, Doc thought, *"Hell, I've done this before. I can make it one more time."*

But had he been honest with himself, he would have known he didn't really care whether he made it or not.

The road was hard to follow. Doc was completely blinded again and again, managing to stay on the road more by instinct than vision. The wind-driven crystals of snow and ice came through the insulation around the windows and doors of the car, forced their way through the heating system and created a snowstorm inside the Chrysler. Doc drove for nearly an hour to cover the fifteen miles across the mountain valley. Ahead of him loomed Kenosha Pass, the steep ascent from the valley floor that would lift him out of South Park, over the mountain and on his way toward Denver. Suddenly a shadow appeared out of the blinding snow—an old pickup truck, buried in the drifting snow at the roadside. A moment later a figure emerged from the truck, pushing hard in an effort to force the door open against the howling wind. Doc's car was moving so slowly that he was only a few feet past the truck before he was stopped. He left the motor idling as he tried to look back up the road toward the truck, but the storm had blotted out all traces of the other vehicle. There was no sign of the figure which had been struggling with the truck door a moment before.

"Oh hell, guess I'd better go look," Doc muttered. "Can't leave him out here. He'd be dead in an hour."

Doc Oliver struggled from the car and fought his way back through the blinding storm. He crept the length of his own car and then lost his footing as the wind struck him with full force, driving him to his knees when he no longer had his car to brace against. The trip back to the truck took several minutes and all of Doc's strength. As he reached the drift in which the old truck was buried, he pulled the door open on the side away from the wind. In the darkness he could see well enough to make out two figures, a woman and a small boy, probably eight or nine.

For a moment they watched one another in silence. Then Doc Oliver shouted over the wind, "Ma'am, what in the world are you doing out here with that boy? The two of you are going to freeze to death!"

"Sister in Denver. . . ." was all Doc caught as the woman shouted a reply in the howling darkness.

"Well, come on. I guess you can't stay here. I'm on my way to Denver. You and the boy can come along with me. Watch the wind. It'll blow you off your feet."

The three fought their way back to Doc's car. Doc carried the little boy in his arms. The woman clung desperately to Doc's arm and clutched the small suitcase which had been lying on the seat of the truck. They fell twice within fifty feet and nearly missed finding Doc's car in the blinding snow. Suddenly a glimpse of the tail lights showed them the way to safety.

Once inside the car, Doc turned to the gasping woman. "What are you doing way out here?"

"On our way to Denver. My sister lives there. The truck slipped off the road, then the engine stopped. We couldn't walk in the wind, so we waited. Then you came along. Thank you. It was so cold."

"Your truck stalled when you got your distributor wet. This fine snow gets into everything. When it gets in the distributor, it melts and fouls out your ignition. No motor, no heater. Too damn cold to be out there very long tonight. Cover up the boy and yourself with some of these blankets. We'd better get going or this car will be fouling out next. And I don't think anybody else will be coming along tonight!"

They set out, moving slowly toward the foot of Kenosha Pass. "Once we get to the top of Kenosha, we'll be above the ground blizzard. The wind just blows the snow down here on the valley floor. Once we get above it, we'll be on our way to Denver on a clear, cold night. Next couple of miles to the pass and the trip up this side are going to be tough. Then we're all right." Doc concentrated on his driving.

The man, woman, and boy traveled on in silence, in a car filled with the roaring wind. They reached the foot of Kenosha and crawled their way up the side of the mountain as fast as the poor visibility permitted. The road was drifted near the point of impassability. Doc was a good mountain driver, he had been in snow like this many times in his life. After plowing through each drift, he fought to pick up a little speed before hitting the next, but the angle of the climb up the pass, plus the drifts, gradually stole all his momentum. The car was stopped halfway up the pass.

Doc Oliver tried again and again to break through. Now that he was stopped, he simply couldn't get started up the pass again. The woman and the little boy sat in frozen silence as Doc finally began turning the car around. With his wheels spinning, he could make almost no progress forward or backward. Each small motion brought the car closer to the edge of the narrow mountain road, with a vertical drop of a thousand feet lying just beyond. The blowing snow made the visibility so bad that Doc couldn't see the road, much less the edge of the cliff, as he jockeyed back and forth. At last he made the turn-around and headed the car back down the pass into the teeth of the storm.

"Sorry, lady. There's no way in hell I can make Kenosha tonight. We've got to go back. Fairplay's fifteen miles away. If this storm doesn't let up, we're in for a real problem."

The woman blanched. "Don't go back, I can't go back. He's there!"

Doc looked the woman right in the eye. "He's there? Oh, I see. You're from somewhere around here, aren't you? Where do you live, anyway?"

The woman sat in silence, head down. Doc continued to fight the road and the storm. Then he spoke. "Look, lady, we're in trouble. I've got to know the closest place to get out of this storm. Now, for the last time, where do you live?"

The boy pointed toward the west and spoke for the first time, in a high frightened little voice, "Up by the butte."

Doc squinted into the night storm. "I know the place. Didn't know anybody was wintering in there. That's one hell of a lot closer than Fairplay. Can't be more than four or five miles. You must have bogged that truck down just after you came out on the main highway. Considering this weather, we'd better make straight for your place."

"I told you," the woman shrieked, "don't go back! I can't go back! He's there."

"Lady, I'm sorry you're having trouble with your husband, or whoever '*he*' is. But you'd better understand something. I can't get over Kenosha. Turning around in this wind has likely got some of this damned snow in the distributor already. This car will probably be stalled pretty soon, if I don't run off in the ditch first. Then we'll be sitting here freezing to death, or trying to walk all the way to Fairplay and getting lost and dead in the snow. You do what you want tomorrow or the next day, but right now you and the boy are going home. It's that or sit here and freeze."

The woman turned toward Doc, her face drained white with anger and fear. "You have no right. This isn't your business."

"Lady, right now that little boy of yours is my business—you're my business. If you want to freeze, that's up to you, but you're not going to freeze yourself or that boy while I'm supposed to be taking care of you."

"You have no right. . . ," her voice trailed off into resigned silence.

"What the hell, lady, I guess I always did run everybody's business. I guess that's what some of them hated about me. Anyway, too late to stop now. Lady, you and that boy are going home. If you have troubles with your husband or somebody, that's not my fault. Right now there's no place else to go. Whatever your trouble is, it's not as bad as being dead."

The three sat in silence as Doc fought his way through the roaring, blinding ground blizzard. Down the pass, across the valley floor, he managed to stay on the road and creep back toward the stalled truck where he had first seen the woman and the boy. The visibility was so bad that Doc almost hit the truck before he realized it was there.

"Well, we made it this far. The turnoff to your place has to be close around here somewhere. Tell me quick, lady. If we get stalled, we won't make it to shelter. Now where's the road to your place?"

All resistance was gone. The danger was now uppermost in the woman's mind as well. "Just about a hundred yards on the right. The house is about a mile up that road."

The turnoff was almost impossible to find in the blinding storm. The boy saw it first. "There it is!" The road was drifted nearly shut, but Doc made the turn from the highway, facing directly into the wind and fighting to keep moving as his rear wheels spun and the back end of the car slithered from side to side. They struggled forward for nearly a thousand yards before the engine sputtered and died. Doc tried frantically to restart, but the fine snow had finally reached the Chrysler's distributor. They were fouled, stopped with no hope of restarting.

Doc Oliver looked around him for a moment. "Wrap up in as many of those blankets as you can, protect your face from the wind. We've got to walk for it, storm or no storm. If we stay here, we'll freeze in an hour without the engine to provide heat."

He wrapped the boy in blankets. "Don't be scared, son. We've got a good chance. Can't be more than a half mile from your place."

"*A half-mile!*" Doc thought to himself. "*Might as well be ten miles. We can hardly move in this ground blizzard. Even if we could move, the odds are that we'll lose our way. You dimwitted old bastard, you've done it now. You're the one that had to go to Denver tonight. Merry Christmas, stupid!*"

Doc opened the car door. "Okay, everybody. Hold tight to one another. Son, get right behind me. Get as close as you can and hold my coat with both hands. Don't let go, no matter what. Ma'am, you hold on to your son from the back. Keep close, hang on. Try to keep your faces out of the wind. Keep peeking out of the edge of your blanket— we've got to see the light from your place. And whatever you do, *don't stop and don't let go.*"

Progress was almost impossible in the blinding, stinging snow, the bitter wind, and the drifts. Doc blazed trail as best he could, but one or another of the group fell again and again as they struggled forward. Doc could not tell whether or not he was on the road. All direction was lost. As he blazed the trail, the wind took his breath away. His heart hammered, he breathed in great gasps, his entire body cried out to stop.

"*We'd better see that light soon, or we won't ever see it,*" Doc thought. The three staggered on, without even knowing whether or not they were moving in the right direction. "*I shouldn't be here anyway, but I am. So now what? I can't go on. Hell, I can't go back—guess I'll have to go on.*"

A moment later, through the blast of snow and ice, Doc thought he saw a light. It vanished as quickly as it came. As Doc staggered on, dragging his little band behind him, the light reappeared through the snow. "*Thank God,*" Doc thought.

It took another ten minutes to struggle the last few yards to the door of the ranch house. Doc didn't stand on ceremony. He opened the door and dragged his charges inside, out of the storm. Covered with snow and ice, exhausted, half-frozen—the man, the woman, and the boy stood in the kitchen of the ranch house gasping for breath. It was past three in the morning. A short, stocky man of about forty rose unsteadily from the kitchen table. "What the hell! Who are you?"

Doc unwrapped the blanket from his face. "Take it easy, mister. Found your family stuck in the snow. Thought they'd be better off inside. Here we are—and damn glad to be here, too!"

The rancher couldn't seem to understand what was happening at first. He swayed a bit and steadied himself with his hands on the table. "My family, you say. Hell, I don't have any family. They're long gone. I'm asking you again, mister. What are you doin' here in the middle of the night?"

Doc Oliver turned to the woman and the boy and began to remove the snow-covered blankets wrapped around the youngster. "I told you, partner—brought your wife and boy back."

"Well, I'll be damned!" The stocky man in the flannel shirt blinked his eyes and reached for the whiskey bottle sitting on the kitchen table. He drank straight from the bottle.

"Join me, mister? This is quite an occasion. Those worthless two run away from home and they're back again before the night's over. Where'd you say you found them? Come here, you two, let me take a look at you."

Neither the woman nor the boy had removed their

coats. They cringed against the kitchen wall, eyes wide with fright in their exhausted faces. Seeing the two for the first time in the light, Doc Oliver saw the face of a woman who had been badly beaten, a woman desperately tired, sick, afraid. He looked back at the rancher as he came around the table.

"Take it easy, mister. Your wife and the boy have had a pretty hard time tonight. Give 'em a break. We were damned lucky to make it up here at all!"

The shorter man stood before Doc. "Mind your own damn business! I didn't ask you to bring 'em back. You come into my place and tell me how to act, what to do. You can go to hell. If you don't like it here, you can leave right now and take these two with you!"

"Look buddy, take it easy. These two can't go anywhere until this storm lets up. They're beat. So am I."

The drunken man flushed, hesitated a moment, then turned toward a gun rack on the wall behind him. Doc Oliver saw what was coming and stepped across the room, reaching the man just as he started to lift a rifle from the rack. The two men struggled. Doc was in his mid-fifties, exhausted from his fight with the storm; the rancher was younger, stronger, but very drunk. They wrestled, fell against the table and crashed heavily to the floor. The rifle clattered free and slid across the floor. As the men fought, Doc rolled free, crawled across the floor to reach the rifle, and rose to his feet as the rancher came at him, head down. Grasping the barrel, Doc swung the rifle and smashed the stock across the side of the younger man's head.

The rancher stayed down. Doc leaned heavily against the wall and struggled to get his breath. The woman and the boy cowered in the farthest corner of the room.

After a moment, Doc knelt to take the pulse of the bloodied, unconscious rancher. He felt a surge of relief as he discovered a strong pulse. "He'll be okay, but he's going to have one hell of a headache when he wakes up."

Looking up at the woman and the boy as they watched him with large eyes, Doc spoke again, "Speaking of waking up, we'd better get out before this one comes to. If we don't, I'll have to hold a gun on him the rest of the night. Any other transportation around here?"

The woman pointed to a set of keys on a pegboard by the door. "Jeep," she said, looking toward the barn outside the house.

Doc didn't hesitate. "Okay, lady, let's go. You and the boy get bundled up. We better be on our way!"

They were out the door in a moment, fighting the blizzard and the drifts all the way to the barn. Inside the barn, the jeep started immediately. "Four wheel drive," Doc noted with satisfaction. "Lady, you should have taken this jeep instead of that old truck. You would have made it a whole lot farther. Anyway, we got some transportation now. I just didn't want to spend the night back there with your friend."

The four-wheel drive helped with the drifts. The storm seemed to be easing up and the visibility was getting a little better. Doc worked his way back down the road, past his stalled car, onto the main highway and on toward Fairplay. The storm was stopping and the wind had almost subsided when the jeep pulled up at the Fairplay Hotel at 4:10 a.m.

"Innkeeper, get out of bed! Charley, you've got business out here," Doc roared as he hammered on the door.

The lights inside the hotel came on. A moment later, a

sleepy Charley opened the door. "Damn you, Doc! Don't you have a home?"

Doc Oliver moved the woman and the boy inside. "We need a hot meal, a bath, some dry clothes and about two days sleep. Just keep score and send me the bill. Call Sheriff Thompson and get him over here. We've got a little business to discuss."

The woman and the boy had eaten, were finally warm clear through and were sitting before the open fire with Doc, Charley, and Sheriff Thompson. Mrs. Thompson had rounded up some clean clothes that would fit the woman and the boy. The youngster had fallen asleep on the couch next to his mother.

Sheriff Thompson cleared his throat. "Don't worry, Ma'am, nobody's going to bother you. Right now that man out at the ranch is stranded in the snow without a car. Before he gets over that big headache, I'll be all over him like fly paper. We'll see how he wants to play it. Whether he makes it a little tangle with the law or a big one is up to him. Either way, he's not going to be bothering you or anybody else. When I get through talking to him, he'll know that for sure. Meanwhile, you're free to come or go as you please. Hope some of those clothes are all right for you and the boy."

The woman spoke, "Thank you, Sheriff. Thank you all. But please don't be too hard on him. We're not married. I came up from Denver of my own free will. We've only been at the ranch a couple of weeks. Things didn't go bad until he started drinking about three days ago. I should never have come. I don't want to hurt anyone. All I really want is to forget the whole thing."

Doc finished his drink. "Tomorrow we'll get on down

the road to Denver, get you and your boy to your sister's place and see if we can get you a fresh start."

"Thank you, Doctor Oliver. I wish my son and I had something to give you in return."

"Lady, I'm the one who should be thanking you. You've given me a precious gift. In fact, until I found the two of you out there in the snow, I had forgotten that such a precious gift still existed. Ma'am, you've given me a reason for living."

Doc turned to put on his coat. "Anyway, it's almost seven in the morning. Time to go to bed. Get some sleep. I'll be by here sometime this afternoon. We can make our plans then. Merry Christmas!"

As Doc left the hotel and trudged toward home, the storm was over. The wind had died down, the sky was clear and cold. The first signs of a new dawn turned the snow drifts to a dazzling field of gold reaching far across the valley.

*"By golly, tomorrow's always another day. That's a blessing that too many people take for granted."*